You're About to Become a

Privileged Woman.

INTRODUCING
PAGES & PRIVILEGES™.

It's our way of thanking you for buying
our books at your favorite retail store.

— GET ALL THIS FREE —

WITH JUST ONE PROOF OF PURCHASE:

◆ **Hotel Discounts** up
to 60% at home and
abroad ◆ **Travel Service**
- Guaranteed lowest
published airfares
plus 5% cash back

$50 VALUE

on tickets ◆ **$25 Travel Voucher**

◆ **Sensuous Petite Parfumerie** collection

◆ **Insider Tips Letter**
with sneak previews
of upcoming books

You'll get a FREE personal card, too.
It's your passport to all these benefits– and to
even more great gifts & benefits to come!

There's no club to join. No purchase commitment. No obligation.

Enrollment Form

☐ *Yes!* I WANT TO BE A *Privileged Woman.*

Enclosed is one *PAGES & PRIVILEGES*™ Proof of Purchase from any Harlequin or Silhouette book currently for sale in stores (Proofs of Purchase are found on the back pages of books) and the store cash register receipt. Please enroll me in *PAGES & PRIVILEGES*™. Send my Welcome Kit and FREE Gifts -- and activate my FREE benefits -- immediately.

More great gifts and benefits to come like these luxurious Truly Lace and L'Effleur gift baskets.

▶ DETACH HERE AND MAIL TODAY! ▶

NAME (please print)

ADDRESS   APT. NO

CITY   STATE   ZIP/POSTAL CODE

PROOF OF PURCHASE
SAMPLE ONLY

Please allow 6-8 weeks for delivery. Quantities are limited. We reserve the right to substitute items. Enroll before October 31, 1995 and receive one full year of benefits.

NO CLUB!
NO COMMITMENT!
Just one purchase brings you great Free Gifts and Benefits!
(More details in back of this book.)

Name of store where this book was purchased_____

Date of purchase_____

Type of store:

☐ Bookstore   ☐ Supermarket   ☐ Drugstore

☐ Dept. or discount store (e.g. K-Mart or Walmart)

☐ Other (specify)_____

Which Harlequin or Silhouette series do you usually read?

Pages & Privileges™

Complete and mail with one Proof of Purchase and store receipt to:

U.S.: *PAGES & PRIVILEGES*™, P.O. Box 1960, Danbury, CT 06813-1960

Canada: *PAGES & PRIVILEGES*™, 49-6A The Donway West, P.O. 813, North York, ON M3C 2E8   **PRINTED IN U.S.A**

"I'm convinced you wanted me for the wrong reasons!"

They faced each other like adversaries.

"What reason could there be?" he demanded hotly, "except for the bond I feel tying me to you—"

"But that's just what I'm saying!" she cried. "This bond isn't just to do with me, Catherine Ward. I'd never be sure that it was me you really wanted, or whether you were trying to relive some dream you once had of Isabel Cardoso!"

Eduardo waved her to the sofa. "I think it is time we exorcise the ghost of Isabel. It is only right you should know her story."

Not sure that she really wanted to, Catherine eyed him uneasily. "Are you sure you want to tell me? I mean, if it's some private family matter...."

Dear Reader,

To me, the most important thing in my own life is my family, with all its warmth and love and loyalties, spiced with the odd squabble or two and a lot of fun. This naturally influences my style of writing, and the strength of relationships are, for me, an essential ingredient to blend with the color, romance and adventure which make a story for you, the supremely important reader, to enjoy.

In *A Family Secret*, I try to convey what I truly believe, that love in its strongest, enduring form overcomes all obstacles, that ultimately it is the strength of family ties which forms the foundation for lasting happiness.

Sincerely,

Catherine George

A FAMILY SECRET
Catherine George

Harlequin Books

TORONTO • NEW YORK • LONDON
AMSTERDAM • PARIS • SYDNEY • HAMBURG
STOCKHOLM • ATHENS • TOKYO • MILAN
MADRID • WARSAW • BUDAPEST • AUCKLAND

To Dona Maria Filomena da Camara
Manoel Reynolds de Abreu Coutinho
and her family,
with grateful thanks

ISBN 0-373-03368-0

A FAMILY SECRET

Copyright © 1992 by Catherine George.

First North American Publication 1995.

CHAPTER ONE

ONCE the slight tension of take-off was over Catherine relaxed, watching misty southern England fall away beneath her as the plane headed for Oporto. In a window-seat next to a young couple too wrapped up in each other to notice, she gave a little wriggle of anticipation at the thought of the holiday ahead.

Some of her friends, Catherine knew, thought her life was one long holiday already. She accepted the teasing amicably enough on the rare occasions when they got together, but firmly defended her decision to see something of the world before settling down. Selling designer dresses on a luxury cruise liner was much harder work than most people realised. Besides, if she hadn't been on board when the ship docked in Lisbon on a sunny day last June, she'd never have run into Ana again.

Catherine, who loved Lisbon best of all the ports of call, had gone ashore as early as she could, sharing a taxi with a couple of girls from the purser's office. While the others drank coffee outside one of the cafés Catherine had wandered away to gaze at the tempting handbags in a shop in the Rua Augusta, and could hardly believe her ears when a husky voice called her name. Exclaiming in delight, she'd spun round to face the small, vivacious person of Ana Maria Barroso, ink-black eyes sparkling under heavy tawny hair, her stylish dress a far cry from the jeans and jerseys of her year in Putney as Catherine's room-mate.

Ana hugged Catherine hard, kissing her on both cheeks, then held her away to gaze at her with joy. '*Que maravilha* to find you here! You are on holiday, *querida*?'

Catherine returned the embrace with equal warmth, explaining she was still working on the cruise liner. 'I'm only ashore for a few hours—the ship sails at five.'

Demanding every moment of Catherine's company before then, Ana paused only long enough for an introduction to the girls from the ship, then swept Catherine off to eat a seafood lunch in the Travessa do Santo Antao, both of them talking non-stop as they filled in the events of the time since they'd parted. Ana had been working very hard since college, helping her brother with his tourist venture, as intended, but now, she informed Catherine, Eduardo was obliged to find a new slave to help him.

'Because I am getting married!' she finished in guileless triumph.

Catherine beamed, toasting her in mineral water. 'Congratulations. But I thought you were dead against marriage.'

Colour flooded Ana's face as she gave a very expressive shrug. '*E verdade, cara*, but I was stupid. I did not know then what I know now.'

'And what's this great truth you've discovered?'

'Love,' answered Ana simply.

'Ah, I see. Who's the lucky man?'

Ana gurgled. 'Carlos da Cunha.'

Catherine frowned. 'But isn't that the man your brother picked out for you in the first place?'

'*E, sim*. But I was furious because Eduardo wished to arrange my marriage. When I rebelled he—how do you say? Washed his hands with me?'

'I see, I see! Once your brother stopped pushing you saw Carlos in a new light.'

'*Exatamente*!' said Ana happily. 'Also I discovered Carlos wished me to help him in his work, Catherine. This changed everything. I love the *turismo* business, you understand. It is so interesting and I meet so many people. It was not my wish to be just a *dona de casa* like my sisters.'

'Is Carlos in the tourist business, then?'

'He trained as *advogado*—lawyer—like Eduardo. But now the parents of Carlos wish to move to Estoril, leaving Carlos at their Quinta da Floresta in the Lima valley. He admires Eduardo's success and wishes to develop his home for guests in the same way.' Ana gave a contented sigh. 'So I told Carlos that if it was a true partnership, if we could work together, I would marry him. Carlos promised on his life that I could do whatever I wish, always. And when he—he——' She stopped dead, the colour rushing to her cheeks again.

Catherine smiled affectionately. 'And when he made love to you that was that.'

'How did you guess?'

'A certain look in your eye, my pet. Quite unmistakable.'

'Only the kisses, you understand,' said Ana with dignity.

Catherine's eyes softened. 'Of course, love.'

'He desires more,' said Ana candidly. 'I also, every time we kiss, but it is not possible. So we wait until a *noite de nupcias*—our wedding night.'

Catherine patted Ana's hand, feeling centuries older instead of a mere month or two. 'I hope you'll be very happy, love.'

'I expect no miracles. I shall work hard at my marriage,' Ana assured her, then demanded all Catherine's news in turn.

'I've started looking out for jobs ashore,' said Catherine, sighing. 'It's time I joined the rat race, I suppose—not that my job on the ship's any picnic, believe me. I'm on my feet for hours on end in the boutique, do the books, arrange fashion shows and try not to get claustrophobia in a tiny cabin shared with another girl. But on the plus side I earn good money, meet a great many interesting people, and get the chance to see something of the world before I settle down.'

'But are you never *enjoada*—seasick?' asked Ana, making a face.

'No, luckily. I can't say I exactly enjoy a life on the ocean wave in a force-ten gale, but there haven't been many of those, fortunately.'

Ana beckoned the waiter to pay the bill, then looked at Catherine questioningly. 'And Dan? You do not speak of him. You are no longer together?'

Catherine's face shuttered. 'No. Once he graduated Dan made it mortifyingly clear there was no place in his future plans for me. So when I heard of the job on the liner I went for it. The travelling was a way of gluing my ego together again.' She shrugged philosophically, shaking back her dark hair. 'And how about you, Ana?' she asked gently. 'Have you come to terms with your own heartache?'

Ana nodded gravely. '*Mais ou menos*. I still grieve, *naturalmente*. But life must go on, *não é*?' She brightened. 'But never shall I forget your kindness when I was so unhappy. To lose my mother and my brother within days of each other was so terrible that without you I would not have recovered from such a blow.' She reached a hand across the table to grasp Catherine's. 'But let us talk of happier things. Now fate has brought us together again, promise you will come to my wedding! Come a week or two sooner and have a little holiday at the Quinta das Lagoas first. I would so love your company. My sisters are always busy with their families.' She made a face. 'I am only here in Lisboa now for the *baptismo* of Leonor's new son. I cannot wait to return to work at home! Say you'll come to stay for a little, *querida*. It would please me so much.'

In the end it had been impossible to refuse. Not that Catherine had any desire to. She'd always been intrigued by Ana's stories of her family, and her home in the Minho in the north of Portugal. Catherine's knowledge of the country was restricted to the periodic dockings in Lisbon on the cruise ship. She had disembarked at Southampton for the final time just the previous week, much to the relief of her mother, who complained of seeing far too little of her globe-trotting daughter. Sometimes they could only manage an hour or two together in Southampton before the ship turned round and headed out to sea again, taking Catherine with it.

The airport at Oporto, minuscule by Heathrow standards, charmed Catherine from the moment she descended from the plane to take the small bus to the Customs building. Glad of her dark glasses, she tied a scarf over her head to protect it from sunshine blazing down in such contrast to the damp, dull

London she'd left behind. As always in Portugal, everyone she spoke to at the airport was courteous and pleasant, including the young man from the car-hire firm, who was waiting for her, to her surprise, when she emerged from the terminal building.

'Miss Ward?' he enquired, indicating the badge on his lapel.

Having expected to go searching for him, Catherine smiled warmly, and in an admirably short time the necessary formalities were completed, the keys to an almost new Ford Fiesta handed over, and Catherine was on her way out of the airport after a few instructions as to the route.

For a while she drove with great care, adjusting to the right-hand drive of the car and what felt like the wrong side of the road. But soon she was driving automatically, able to spare attention for the scenery along the route which followed the coast from Oporto to Viana do Castelo and on to Valença do Minho.

Catherine had been deliberately vague about her time of arrival to Ana and felt no compulsion to hurry. Something in the very air of rural Portugal made a nonsense of any urgency. She soon settled to a speed leisurely enough to appreciate her surroundings as she passed groups of smiling pedestrians on the walkways at the side of the road, carts loaded with barrels of grapes and drawn by oxen with lyre-shaped horns and carved wooden yokes, their attendants often sturdy, brown-skinned women who paced beside in an un-hurried way totally in keeping with the sun-drenched landsape. Catherine sighed with pleasure. Life had been hectic for a long time. Before she tackled the next phase of her career she intended to enjoy this unexpected interlude in Portugal to the full.

After an hour or so Catherine felt a leap of excitement as the signpost marked Pontalegre finally came into view. The last lap of her journey led her off the main highway on a road which meandered along the banks of the River Lima through a landscape drenched with sunlight. Time seemed at a standstill in the sleepy little villages along the route, some of them no more than handfuls of small dwellings clustered near a church.

Catherine had no trouble in finding the Quinta das Lagoas, which was easily recognisable by the imposing arched gateway set in walls which lined the road. She signalled a right turn, waited for a lorry to come trundling by, then steered the car carefully through the arch and along a narrow gravelled track. As she approached the house her eyes widened behind the lenses of her aviator glasses. Ana had described Quinta das Lagoas as a farm, but to Catherine it looked more like a small stately home, complete with turreted tower and a second archway giving on to a courtyard at the back. As she passed from brilliant sunlight to the ebony shadow cast by the house Catherine found herself temporarily unsighted as she tried to negotiate the second, narrower archway. To her horror she found herself suddenly nose to nose with a battered pick-up. She slammed on the brakes hard, her head whipping back with a sickening crack as the car halted inches from the other vehicle.

While Catherine saw stars for a moment the door was wrenched open, her seatbelt released and deft hands lifted her from the car to set her on her feet. Catherine's faculties took a moment or two to sort themselves out before informing her she was in contact with a hard male body which radiated heat and dust and a tang of clean sweat. She disengaged herself hurriedly, giddy and embarrassed as she tried to smile at her rescuer, whose looks, even to someone in her present dazed state, were noticeably spectacular. Runnels of sweat ran down his dusty face from his damp, curling hair, he was bare to the waist, and his torso bronzed and muscular above ancient denims torn at the knees. He was also saying something urgent and rapid, she realised, her dazed brain unable to dredge up any phrase-book Portuguese to decipher it.

'*Desculpe-me*,' she croaked, her face hot as she saw a knot of similarly dressed men looking on with interest in the background. Rescue came in the form of a cry of delight from the gallery running round the upper floor of the building. Ana came hurtling down the stairs to embrace Catherine, voluble with apologies for not being ready to greet her, at the same time issuing a flood of unintelligible scolding to the man regarding them with a wry smile on his dirty face. Ana waved him away with shooing movements as she hurried her guest up the staircase and into a reception hall which drove all thoughts of the incident from Catherine's head.

'Welcome to Quinta das Lagoas,' cried Ana happily.

Catherine gazed in undisguised awe at a marble-floored chamber with wooden ceiling and white-plastered walls hung with oil-paintings and exquisite ceramic plates. A suit of armour stood between two deep window embrasures, straight-backed leather chairs heavy with studs were ranged against the walls, and in the centre of the room stood a refectory table with a runner embroidered with armorial bearings, a bronze candelabrum at one end, a pile of ancient, leather-bound books at the other.

'How do you like my home, Catherine?' asked Ana eagerly. 'Do you feel better now? Have you had a good flight? Did you manage to find your way, *querida*? I have been worrying! You should have let me send someone to fetch you——'

'Stop, stop!' protested Catherine, laughing. 'Your home is magnificent, love, and I had a very good flight, and I enjoyed the drive up here very much. Pity I had to ruin my entrance like that!'

'You are sure you're not hurt? No? Then let me show you the house——'

'Ana!' A sturdy, middle-aged woman appeared in the doorway, her face reproachful. '*Espera*!'

Ana smiled affectionately. 'This is Maria Fernanda, Catherine, who has been with us forever.'

Catherine smiled and held out her hand. 'How do you do?'

'*Muito prazer*,' returned the woman, looking pleased as she took the hand. '*Bemvindo*—welcome to Quinta das Lagoas.'

'She is a tyrant and rules us all!' said Ana dramatically, putting an affectionate arm about the woman's shoulders.

'*Bobagem*!' protested Fernanda, and patted Ana's hand. 'Your guest must be tired. Take Dona Caterina to her room, then bring her to the *sala* for the English tea before showing her the rest of the house.'

'*Sim, senhora*!' Ana saluted pertly, then took Catherine by the hand, leading her to a granite staircase which spiralled upwards from one corner of the room.

'We have no *turistas* here now until after the wedding,' she said, as she preceded Catherine up two winding flights of stairs. 'So we have put you in the honeymoon suite on the top floor of the tower, *querida*.'

'Goodness, how splendid!' Catherine exclaimed in delight as she followed Ana into a charming room dominated by a bed with a headboard carved from rosewood in a convoluted pattern of vine leaves and grapes, the design repeated in green on the white curtains at the windows. The tower-room commanded a magnificent view of the entire Quinta, looking out over a vista of vines grown upward over pillars in an endless succession of pergolas to allow for the corn and vegetables planted in the soil beneath. Nearer the house bougainvillaea rioted in a purple frame around the outbuildings in the courtyard, the entire scene bathed in the honeyed warmth of the afternoon sun.

Leaning at the open window, Catherine gazed, fascinated, breathing in air untainted by anything other than the perfume of flowers and earth and vegetation. She turned back to Ana in wonder. 'It's utterly beautiful here. How on earth did you manage in England, exchanging all this for our fog and rain and crowds?'

'There were many advantages,' Ana assured her, smiling. She opened a door in the corner of the room. 'Here is your own bathroom. Eduardo and I sleep in the new bedrooms on the ground floor, where the wine was once stored, Fernanda and her husband Manoel in the rooms outside in the *patio*.'

'So I'm all alone up here?'

'*Sim*.' Ana looked doubtful. 'Do you mind? There are other rooms——'

'Mind?' Catherine hugged the other girl in delight. 'I've spent most of my time lately cooped up in a tiny cabin with another girl, with no room to swing a cat. This, my cherub, is paradise!'

After Ana left Catherine took off her sunglasses and unwound the scarf, eager to wash the effects of the journey away before brushing her heavy black hair until it shone, hanging heavy and straight to her shoulders. She tucked her striped pink shirt neatly into her jeans, then went slowly down the stone stairs, marvelling at the thickness of the walls as she descended to the hall, where Ana was waiting to escort her through a pair of wooden doors heavy with iron studs.

'You must be longing for some tea, Catherine. We shall drink it in here as Fernanda commands!' Her face expectant, she led Catherine into the *sala*, which was larger, but less daunting than the hall, despite a great cowled stone fireplace and dark curtains heavy with crimson braid and more armorial embroidery. Deep sofas and easy chairs were grouped around a low table in front of the fireplace, carved chests and side-tables stood against the walls, with bowls of fresh flowers and dozens of framed photographs everywhere.

'It is too warm today for a fire,' apologised Ana, as she installed Catherine on a sofa. 'Unless you are cold, of course,' she added anxiously.

'Cold?' Catherine laughed. 'Stop fussing. Oh, Ana, what a room. I can't believe you let this place to tourists!'

'But we do. And so far it has always been treated with respect. Only three *quartos*—bedrooms—are available in the house, you understand. Yours, and the other two on the floor below you in the tower. But there are the *casas de campo*, the cottages outside in the *patio*. Those who stay there are welcome to come inside to the *sala* in the evenings if they wish.'

Catherine was deeply impressed. 'If this place were mine I don't think I could bear to give strangers the run of it.'

'If you needed the money you would,' said Ana prosaically. 'Without the income from *turismo* it would be very hard to maintain either the Quinta or the town house in Pontalegre.'

They would be moving to the Casa das Camelias in town for the wedding, she informed Catherine. 'We have visitors there at the moment, but next week we shall have it to ourselves, to prepare for the *dia do casamento*.' She gave a sudden, excited laugh. '*Meu Deus, querida*, can you believe it? Soon I shall be a wife!'

'*Se Deus quizer*. How I pray for your husband!' teased Fernanda, arriving with a teapot and a large cake on a silver plate.

'He does not need your prayers! Besides,' added Ana cheerfully, 'Senhora da Cunha has left her cook with us, so Carlos will not starve.'

Fernanda laughed indulgently. 'He will not care about food for a while with you as his bride, *carinha*. Now fetch the toast, *por favor*.'

Ana jumped up, grinning at Catherine. 'She thinks the English cannot survive without toast at every meal!'

While she was gone Catherine won Fernanda's approval by asking about the various photographs in the room, and with alacrity Fernanda escorted her on a tour of sepia-tinted studies of long-dead Barrosos. The photograph in pride of place in an elaborate silver frame, she informed the guest proudly, was a signed portrait of King Manoel II of Portugal. Her face softened as she pointed out a study of Ana's mother as a bride, all pearls and lace and lilies.

'The Condessa's *vestido de casamento* was so beautiful,' said Fernanda, with a disapproving look at Ana as the girl returned. 'But this child refuses to wear white, like her mother and sisters before her.'

'What's your dress like, then, Ana?' asked Catherine, intrigued.

'Black,' said Ana, grinning all over her face.

'*Black*?'

'*Preto, mesmo*,' said Fernanda acidly. 'This child insists on a Minhota wedding, like a peasant!'

'*Que snob*, Fernanda!' scolded Ana. 'It will be such fun! I shall be in black all hung with gold ornaments and I shall wear a white veil and white knitted stockings and black clogs and I have persuaded Carlos to wear the black suit and embroidered shirt of all Minhoto *noivos*. And my bridesmaids will be dressed just like me. You will love it, *querida*!'

Catherine agreed, laughing. 'I certainly will— remind me to buy lots of extra film for my camera. How ordinary I'll be in my humdrum suit and hat!'

'I think it would be very difficult for you to look ordinary,' said Ana simply.

'*E verdade*,' agreed Fernanda. 'Ana has told me much about you, Dona Caterina, but I did not expect an English rose to possess such colouring. You could be one of us!'

'Praise indeed!' said Ana, when they were alone. 'Fernanda is not one for the flattery.'

'I'm honoured.'

'Perhaps it surprises you to find a servant so—so familiar, but Fernanda came here as my nurse when

I was born, you see,' explained Ana. 'When I went to school she gradually took on more and more until now she is not only *governanta*—housekeeper?—but also cook and general tyrant of Quinta das Lagoas. Eduardo is the only one who commands any respect from her.'

'But it's easy to see she adores you, Ana.'

'*Pois é!*' agreed Ana, wickedly. 'It is because I am so adorable, *nao é*?'

'And modest!' Catherine laughed as she took the cup of tea Ana offered. 'Lovely; I was dying for this. By the way, I must get my things out of the car.' She made a face. 'I hope your wedding present survived the trauma of my arrival!'

'So do I,' agreed Ana fervently. 'It has probably been taken to your room with the rest of your luggage by now.'

'By the sexy farmhand who pulled me out of the car?' asked Catherine, grinning.

Ana frowned, puzzled. 'Sexy——?' She broke off, dissolving into helpless giggles as a man appeared in the doorway at the far end of the room.

Catherine's heart sank as the farmhand in question strolled towards them, torn jeans replaced by pale linen trousers and a silk shirt. Now the sweat and dust were gone, and Catherine's faculties functioning normally, his likeness to Ana was obvious. But this face was more aquiline, the features carved by a heavier hand, the brows not only more marked but raised in amusement. As he strolled down the room towards them it was obvious he'd heard every word. But even as Catherine was bracing herself to make an apology he stopped dead in his tracks, his smile of greeting frozen in his handsome face. There was a brief electric silence while Eduardo Barroso forgot his manners entirely. He stared, stunned, his dark eyes incredulous, until at last, at a sharp admonition from Ana in Portuguese, he pulled himself together with palpable effort, giving Catherine a formal bow.

'Catherine, this is my brother,' said Ana, frowning blackly at him. 'You have already met, of course. I refused to introduce him to you earlier because he was so dirty. Miss Catherine Ward, may I present Eduardo Duarte de Abreu Barroso, Conde de Pontalegre?'

CHAPTER TWO

SLIGHTLY stunned to learn that Ana's brother possessed a title, Catherine held out her hand.

'*Muito prazer*,' she said, smiling politely. 'I hope
that's correct?'

Eduardo Barroso took her hand and bent to raise
it to within a fraction of his lips before releasing it,
his face schooled to smooth courtesy by the time he
straightened. 'Perfectly correct,' he said, in English
as good as Ana's. 'But the pleasure is mine, Miss
Ward. I am enchanted to meet you at last. It has long
been my desire to express my thanks for your kindness
to Ana in her time of grief.'

His voice was musical, with an attractive huskiness
to it, but to Catherine his little speech lacked spon-
taneity, as though he'd rehearsed it in advance.

'I did very little.' She hesitated. 'Ana has never
mentioned your title, by the way. To avoid even more
embarrassing mistakes on part perhaps you'd tell me
the correct way to address you.'

A smile of great charm transformed his bronzed
face, the formality suddenly vanished. 'By my name,
por favor. The title is no longer used, except on legal
documents. Ana was playing games.' He shook his
head reprovingly at his sister, who shrugged, unrepentant, very obviously relieved to find him in normal
command of himself again.

'*I* was playing games! And what of you, Eduardo?'
she demanded bluntly. 'You looked amazed at the

22

sight of Catherine. *Por que*? I have told you often enough how lovely she is!'

'Even so,' he said silkily, leaning against the chimney-piece, 'I was not prepared for such beauty.'

'*Bobagem*, Eduardo. It was more than that!'

Eduardo passed a hand over hair as tawny as Ana's now it was dry. 'It is nothing sinister, I promise.' He gave his sister a quelling look. 'It is just that by some strange coincidence Miss Ward greatly resembles a lady I once knew.'

'*Quem*?' demanded Ana.

His face set. 'It was before you were born, *querida*.'

Ana shook her head impatiently. '*Nossa Senhora*, Eduardo, must you be so mysterious?'

Catherine decided this was a good moment to make herself scarce. 'Perhaps you'd both excuse me for a while? I'd like to unpack and have a bath before dinner.'

'Our house is yours, Miss Ward,' Eduardo assured her. 'While you are here please feel free to do as you wish. Later, when you come down, perhaps you will try some of our famous white port as an aperitif before dinner.'

'Thank you. I'll enjoy that very much.' She smiled at him composedly, then gave Ana a swift hug. 'I'll see you later, then.'

'Take as long as you wish, *querida*,' said Ana. 'Dinner will wait on your pleasure. Shall I see you to your room?'

Catherine assured her that she could find her way alone, and left brother and sister together, pretty sure that Eduardo Barroso was still suffering from shock at the sight of her, despite the charming smile and his polished bow as he held the door open for her. To know she had a double was an oddly creepy sensation. As she climbed the worn, shadowy stairs to her room Catherine felt grateful for the modern electric lamps set into sconces which had once held torches to light the way.

After her gaffe at mistaking Eduardo for one of his own workers Catherine was glad of the respite alone as she stowed her belongings away in the carved wardrobe and chests. Afterwards she opened Ana's wedding present gingerly to inspect the six antique porcelain 'trios', eighteenth-century Spode coffee and teacups which shared a single saucer, as was the custom when they were manufactured. Relieved to find they showed no signs of damage in their nests of polythene bubble-wrap, Catherine went off to run a bath among the blue and yellow Portuguese tiles of the modern bathroom, wondering what to wear for her first dinner at Quinta das Lagoas.

Her job aboard the cruise ship had meant that Catherine could occasionally buy designer clothes at greatly reduced prices, resulting in a marked improvement in her wardrobe. Something to be grateful for, she thought wryly, now she'd seen Ana's home— and met Ana's brother.

With Eduardo Barroso's casual elegance in mind Catherine went through her clothes later with close attention, her face suddenly hot at the thought that in some ways his impact had been greater at their first encounter, bare chest and sweat included. She dismissed the thought impatiently, along with her original intention of wearing a white cotton sweater and navy linen trousers. Instead she took out a black silk shirt printed with rectangles of white and knotted the ends at the waist of a narrow white skirt, added a heavy silver bangle, secured her hair behind her ears with a pair of silver-mounted combs, then made up her face with the skill she'd learned from one of the girls in the beauty salon on the liner.

As she gave herself a final, considering scrutiny in the mirror Catherine shook her head wryly. She was, she realised, taking rather more trouble than usual to look her best. And no prizes for guessing why. The legendary Eduardo, subject of many of Ana's out-pourings, had long been the subject of Catherine's curiosity. Meeting with him at last had not been the anticlimax anticipated. In the flesh he was even more charismatic than the picture his doting sister had painted. The title had come as rather a shock, it was true—not that it made a scrap of difference to someone like ordinary Catherine Ward. The Conde de Pontalegre, whether he used the title or not, had probably been promised since birth to some local heiress with a pedigree to match.

When Catherine arrived downstairs with the box of china and a carrier bag containing gifts bought on the plane, Eduardo Barroso was alone in the *sala*. As Catherine had anticipated, he was now wearing a jacket, and had knotted a tie at the collar of his silk shirt.

'*Meu Deus*, why did you not ask me to help, Miss Ward?' He sprang up to relieve her of her burden. 'This is heavy.' He frowned as he set the box down on a table.

'Not really. Just awkward.' Catherine smiled. 'You've no idea what a nuisance it was on the plane. I sat with it on my knee, much to the steward's dis-approval. I was afraid to let it out of my sight!'

'Is it so precious, then?'

'It's Ana's wedding present—and *very* fragile. My mother thought I was mad to buy something so impractical to bring by air.'

'But you could not be dissuaded!'

'No.' She shrugged ruefully. 'It's one of my more maddening attributes. I'm obstinate as a mule about some things.'

'But so very much more beautiful!' He looked at her with unnerving intensity, his eyes frank in their admiration as they lingered long enough to make her restive. He smiled in apology. '*Perdõeme.* I did not mean to stare. But now I have time to study your face more closely I am much reassured.'

She eyed him quizzically. 'In what way?'

'Because I have discovered that your eyes are the colour of honey, or perhaps amber——'

'And that's of significance?'

Eduardo Barroso inclined his head. 'The lady you resemble so greatly had grey eyes, of a clarity like raindrops. Come,' he added, gesturing towards the sofa. 'Let me give you a glass of the promised port wine. Ana has gone to bathe and change, a process which can take much time, as you may remember. I have asked Fernanda to serve dinner a little later tonight.' He smiled as he filled two glasses from a decanter. 'Fernanda argued, as is her way, but I knew you would prefer to dine up here informally, rather than in the *sala de jantar* downstairs, which is more suitable for a large gathering.'

'You were right.' Catherine tasted the wine appreciatively. 'That's *very* good. But I thought port was a drink you Portuguese exported to my country rather than drank yourselves.'

He shrugged and sat down in the chair nearest the sofa. 'Some of us have a taste for it. But it is the tawny port we shall drink after the meal which is considered "the cure for all ills save death" by my countrymen. You shall judge for yourself later.'

For a moment or two they chatted politely, like any couple only recently acquainted. Eduardo questioned Catherine about her journey, and her opinion of the countryside she'd driven through, then apologised for his disreputable state at their first encounter. 'Also I feared so much that you were hurt, my English deserted me.'

'It's I who should apologise,' Catherine assured him. 'I just didn't see you coming the other way in the truck.'

'But the *camião* was stationary!' He looked amused. 'I had that very moment moved it out of the way—as I thought—to leave room for your car. Ana should have told you to drive around the house to the back to reach the *patio*. It is very difficult to drive through the inner arch, even in a small car.'

'Oh, I see.' Catherine shook her head. 'Stupid of me. I'm lucky the brakes were good on the car.'

'And your reactions so quick! You are quite sure you suffered no hurt?'

'My neck's a bit sore,' she admitted, 'but nothing to make a fuss about.'

'Ah! The British dislike fuss, *não é*?'

'I can't answer for the rest, but this one does.'

One of Eduardo's dark, arched eyebrows rose. 'I shall do my best to remember that.'

Catherine looked away, occupying herself with finishing her wine.

'May I give you more, Miss Ward?'

'No, thank you.' Catherine looked up at him challengingly. 'And if you stick to "Miss Ward", Senhor Conde, I'll feel obliged to address you by your title.'

'Then of course I shall be delighted to use your given name,' he said promptly.

There was a short pause while they took stock of each other, then Eduardo set down his glass on a small table with a decisive click. 'You are very tactful, Catherine.'

'Tactful?'

One of his eyebrows rose mockingly. 'You have not commented on my lamentable behaviour when we met here earlier. I assure you it is not my way to greet guests in such a fashion!'

'I didn't imagine it was.'

'Do you not wish to know why?'

'I do, naturally, but please don't feel obliged to tell me if you'd rather not.'

Eduardo's eyes shadowed. 'One day I shall tell the entire story. For the moment perhaps it is enough for you to know that you bear a remarkable resemblance to a beautiful girl I knew when I was young. Isabel Cardoso was a relative who came to make her home with us. She died a long time ago, before Ana was even born.'

'You must have been *very* young!'

'I was twelve, and she, *coitada*, only eighteen.'

'But you cared for her very much,' said Catherine gently.

'She was my first love, *sem duvida*,' he agreed sombrely, a look of relief on his face when Ana came dashing into the room, glowing with happiness after a telephone call from Carlos.

'*Como vai*, you two,' she cried. 'Carlos sends greetings to my English friend, and Fernanda is asking if she may serve dinner.'

'She may indeed,' said Eduardo, jumping up. 'It is late. Catherine must be hungry after her tiring day.'

Catherine, however, found her previous enthusiasm for dinner slightly dampened by Eduardo's information. Fortunately some time elapsed before they actually began to eat, due to the spirited conversation conducted by Fernanda as she went to and fro, laying the small round table near the window with heavy silver and beautiful old porcelain. By the time the first course finally put in an appearance Catherine's slight feeling of melancholy had given way to the anticipation her bowl of steaming *caldo verde* merited.

'You have eaten this soup before?' asked Eduardo as he held her chair for her.

'No, never. On my brief forays into Lisbon I tended to eat fish if I had time for a meal.' Catherine smiled up at him, grateful for the change to everyday conversation after the drama of his story.

'Fernanda left the *chourico*—smoked garlic sausage—out of the soup tonight,' Ana informed Catherine. 'In deference to our English guest the only ingredients are cabbage and potato and her secret witch's spell for seasoning it!'

'Ridiculous child,' said Eduardo. 'Is it to your taste, Catherine?'

She assured him it was very much so, as was the main course of crisp chicken grilled with rosemary and lemon.

'I think Fernanda must be a witch,' she commented after tasting it. 'She's certainly put a magic spell on this wonderful chicken.'

'And to complete the magic,' said Eduardo smoothly, filling her wine glass, 'since this is your first visit to the Minho the wine is, of course, *vinho verde*.'

'Is this from your own grapes?' asked Catherine, liking the light, fresh taste.

Ana nodded. 'From the best year of the past decade, *não é*, Eduardo?'

'I was saving it for a special occasion,' he said, raising his glass to Catherine.

'I'm flattered!' She smiled, flushing a little. 'You own a lot of land. Do you market the wine?'

To her surprise he explained that only a few hectares of the land surrounding the Quinta were actually his own province. The rest was parcelled out to *rendeiros*—men who paid rent to cultivate individual plots of vines and corn and various vegetables.

'It was different in my father's time,' he went on. 'The entire Quinta das Lagoas, along with Casa das Camelias in Pontalegre, was his inheritance. When my father died Pedro, by law, could inherit only a maximum third of the property.' A shadow passed across his face. 'Now *I* am heir to a third, the rest divided between my sisters.'

Ana's eyes softened in sympathy. 'Eduardo never expected to inherit the title, Catherine. When—when Pedro and my mother died so suddenly he was a— how do you say?—up-and-coming lawyer in Lisboa.'

'No longer. Now I am a *mistura* of hotelier, farmer and mechanic,' said Eduardo without self-pity. '*E vida mesmo*—it is life. We must take what it gives and do our best with it, *não é*?'

Catherine raised her glass to him in toast. 'I'll drink to that. My sentiments exactly.'

As the three of them touched glasses ceremoniously Fernanda came in to remove the gratifyingly empty plates. She smiled, pleased, when Catherine told her the meal was wonderful, accepting the praise with pride as she set down a bowl of perfect fresh fruit, a large wedge of cheese which Catherine took to be Brie, and a basket of crusty, feather-light rolls.

'Try some of the cheese, Catherine,' advised Eduardo. 'It is from the heights of the Sierra d'Estrela, something of a—a treat?—because the sheep from which it comes can only graze when the snows have melted.'

Catherine liked the cheese very much, also the newly baked roll eaten with it, and to her surprise even found room for the orange Eduardo peeled for her with a skill she watched in admiration as his slim, strong hands performed the small rite.

'How does Fernanda speak such amazingly good English?' she asked.

'Did Eduardo not tell you?' queried Ana. 'After Isabel Cardoso died—the girl you resemble so closely, Eduardo tells me—my father engaged an English lady as a governess for my sisters.'

Eduardo nodded. 'My mother is of English descent. It has always been a tradition to speak at least some English in the family. Therefore when Isabel— when a new governess was needed my mother had the brainwave and asked Mrs Dent if she would care for the post.'

Mrs Laura Dent, the childless widow of a British regular army man who had brought her to Pontalegre on his retirement, had been only too happy to lavish all her untapped wealth of love and care—and discipline—on the Barroso children.

Ana laughed. 'She was already a fixture by the time I was born, but she would never abandon her house and move in with us altogether. She insisted on her independence and retained her own home until she died.'

'A lady after my own heart,' commented Catherine.

'And *very* energetic,' said Eduardo, smiling reminiscently. 'It was not enough to teach English to my sisters and myself. Dona Laura soon had most of the younger servants fairly fluent too, especially Fernanda. Only Pedro, away at Coimbra, escaped Dona Laura's attentions. My mother, of course, was deeply thankful to have an elderly lady in charge of the children after——' He stopped, his face suddenly shuttered, and changed the subject to talk of wedding plans, which achieved the intended effect, since it banished all thought of Isabel, and Catherine's extraordinary resemblance to her, from Ana's head for the rest of the evening.

When they left the table to drink coffee in the chairs grouped before the great fireplace Catherine handed over the wedding present to a delighted Ana, along with a duty-free bottle of perfume. Rather more diffidently she presented Eduardo with a bottle of Glenlivet whisky.

Ana flung her arms round Catherine and gave her a smacking kiss before turning her attention to her gifts. Eduardo, although more restrained, gave Catherine a smile of unnerving intimacy as he raised her hand to his lips, this time making deliberate contact with her skin before he straightened, expressing his thanks.

'I trust it's a brand you like?' she said breathlessly, utterly astonished by the fire streaking through her veins from the place where his lips had touched her skin.

'I had not expected a gift,' he said absently, openly fascinated by her vivid blush. 'You are most kind.'

'A mere token of appreciation for having me here!'

Ana gave a squeal of joy as she held up a pair of cups, exclaiming over the beauty of the white porcelain banded in dark blue and gold.

'You were forever drinking tea and coffee in Putney!' Catherine turned to her with a smile. 'It seemed the most appropriate present. I hope you don't have boxes of the stuff already?'

Ana replaced the cups reverently so that she could hug Catherine. 'None as exquisite as this!'

'Nor as valuable,' remarked Eduardo percipiently. 'Eighteenth-century, Catherine, are they not?'

'*Circa* eighteen hundred, anyway,' she agreed. 'Perhaps some day I'll track down a cream jug and sucrier to go with them. At the moment this was all I could match up.'

'*And* afford, you extravagant girl,' said Ana. 'I must take one to show Fernanda, then I will ring Carlos to tell him. *Com licença, querida.*' She raced away, her scarlet cotton skirt fluttering.

'I was about to ask indulgence for her youth,' remarked Eduardo drily. 'But it occurred to me that you and Ana were students together, which means you cannot be much older.'

Catherine eyed him, amused. 'Do I look so much older, then?'

Eduardo held out his cup for more coffee. 'Not older, exactly. More mature, *não é*? An adult, self-sufficient young lady, if you will forgive me.'

'My mother says I was born grown up.' Catherine's eyes shadowed. She changed the subject quickly, saying the first thing which came into her head, which was to ask why Isabel Cardoso had died so young.

'She drowned herself,' said Eduardo quietly.

Catherine stared at him in horror. 'Oh, I'm so sorry—I wouldn't have asked——'

'Isabel was driven to it by unrequited love,' he went on, almost as though he hadn't heard her.

'What a terrible thing!'

'*E verdade.*' He looked up, his eyes quizzical. 'You find it hard to understand a girl who kills herself for such a reason, Catherine?'

'I'm afraid I do.'

'What is your cure for such a problem?'

Her mouth tightened. 'My hypothetical sufferer simply finds work which takes her as far away as possible from the object of her infatuation, to ensure swift and complete recovery.'

Eduardo's eyes narrowed. 'And does this hypothetical woman of yours succeed in her aim?'

'You really do speak my language well.'

'Which does not answer my question.'

'Oh, yes,' said Catherine casually. 'She gets over it.'

'I am glad.'

'Ana has told you, then, that—that I once had great expectations?'

'Ah, how literary we are. Now we proceed from Shakespeare to Dickens, Dona Laura's favourite author,' said Eduardo smiling.

'I'm impressed.'

He hesitated. 'Forgive me if I trespass, Catherine, but Ana told me that you had a *noivo* when you were in college. Is this true?'

'It was. At least I thought so.' Catherine shrugged. 'But once we graduated Dan couldn't wait to plunge into the big business jungle. There was no place in his plans for me.'

Casually, as though unaware he was doing so, Eduardo took possession of her hand, his dark eyes grim. 'Did the gentleman achieve success in this jungle of his?'

'Oh, yes. The perfect milieu for a man without scruples, like Dan.' Catherine's mouth took on a cynical twist. 'With hindsight I can see what a fool I was. But at the time I was studying hard and was too naïve and inexperienced to realise my girlish passion was not entirely reciprocated. Not enough for marriage, anyway.'

'You cared very much for him?'

'I cared, yes.'

'And now?'

'Now I'm older, hopefully wiser, and care no more.' Gently she detached her hand, before he could sense that his touch was unsettling her. Having made a fool of herself once, it was no part of her plan to do so a second time, particularly over a man like Eduardo Barroso, who, fascinating and charismatic though he might be, was even less eligible as far as she was concerned than Dan Harrison, boy wonder of the marketing world.

The return of Ana put an end to a conversation which was becoming far too personal for Catherine's peace of mind. Shortly afterwards Eduardo excused himself regretfully, with the plea of work to do in his study, leaving the two girls together to bridge the time since their college days.

'I thought your brother was married,' said Catherine untruthfully at one stage, yielding to her own curiosity.

'He should be,' said Ana. 'Women find him very attractive. Do you?' she added abruptly, eyes dancing.

'Very,' said Catherine honestly.

Ana nodded proudly. 'There have been many women in his life, *de certeza*. One of them, Antonia Soares, stays most constant.' She made a face. 'The death of my mother and Pedro caused much—much upheaval? That is right? Eduardo's life was dramatically changed.'

The responsibility of the Quinta das Lagoas and the town house, far from a blessing, descended like a hair shirt on Eduardo Barroso's elegant shoulders, partly because of his career, and partly because the money which went with his inheritance was insufficient to maintain the family properties in their existing form.

'Both houses had been in the family for two hundred years,' explained Ana. 'To keep them Eduardo was forced to lease some of the land to *rendeiros*, also to accept a grant from the government to develop the houses for *turismo de habitação*. This is accommodation for guests in private homes like these, you understand. To receive the grant he must go on providing this accommodation for ten years from the—the commencement.'

To implement the scheme Eduardo Barroso had been obliged to abandon his legal career, though, as Ana pointed out wryly, his training had not been wasted. When he set about securing his birthright it spared the expense of a legal adviser for the countless problems he was forced to solve.

Catherine was impressed. She admired a man prepared to adapt his life so drastically when it came to the crunch. 'And what about the lady?' she couldn't help asking.

'Antonia?' Ana shrugged. 'Eduardo does not confide in me. Perhaps if Eduardo had remained in Lisboa they would be married by now. I think she does not wish to abandon her career in Lisbon. She is a lawyer also, you see, clever and very handsome— shiny and sharp, like a sword. She comes here very rarely, *gracas a Deus*. But Eduardo sometimes spends a few days in Lisboa.'

Catherine received the news with resignation. 'Is she coming to the wedding?'

'Oh, yes. I had to invite her, you understand.' Ana smiled as Catherine yawned. '*Coitada*, you are tired. Let us say goodnight to Eduardo, then you shall go to bed.'

Eduardo Barroso's study was off the entrance hall. When Ana ushered Catherine into the room he was absorbed in a pile of legal documents. He looked up absently, then leapt to his feet, his smile warm for Catherine.

'We have come to say goodnight, Eduardo,' announced Ana. 'Catherine is tired.'

'It would surprise me if she were not!'

'Just show Catherine the chapel first,' urged Ana.

Catherine's heart sank. She felt bone weary, with no inclination for further exploring. But to her surprise Eduardo merely led the way across the room to the far wall. He waved Catherine to a crimson velvet

prayer stool positioned before a grille low down in the
wall. As Catherine knelt he pressed a switch and she
gasped in wonder as lights came on far below in a
chapel with walls half-tiled in the now familiar
azulejos. From her vantage-point at the grille she
looked down on an impressive carved altar sur-
mounted by a pietà, with half-size figures of Christ
in his mother's arms.

Catherine stared in utter silence, grateful when Ana
came to lean at her shoulder to explain that the grille
was for pregnant ladies of the household, or for in-
valids too infirm to join in the mass below.

Eduardo switched off the light then helped
Catherine up. 'You are very quiet, Catherine.'

'Because I'm so impressed. It's very beautiful.' And
daunting, she thought secretly. She wasn't used to
households where a private chapel was taken for
granted. 'Will you be married there, Ana?'

'Oh, no. It is not big enough. The ceremony will
be in the Igreja Matriz in Pontalegre.'

'And now,' said Eduaro firmly, 'you must let your
guest go to bed, Ana. *Boa noite*, Catherine.' He raised
her hand to his lips, invoking a reaction to his touch
as clamorous and shocking as before. '*Dorme bem*.'

But in the tower-room later Catherine found sleep
elusive. All the new impressions of the day kept her
brain alert, occupied, however hard she tried to
dismiss him, with thoughts of Eduardo Barroso. She
tossed and turned restlessly, dismayed by his unsettling ability to send her hormones running riot with
a single glance from those black eyes of his, let alone
the kisses he pressed on her hand.

Catherine clasped her hands behind her head,
frowning at the starlit sky as she thought of his re-

action to the first sight of her face minus the disguising scarf and glasses. Her resemblance to this Isabel of his had shocked him rigid. And Eduardo Barroso, Catherine felt sure, was normally fairly shockproof. She shivered involuntarily. Knowing she had a double, and a dead one at that, was a strange sensation. Yet on the plus side it had certainly broken the ice. Her likeness to the dead, lamented Isabel had put her on far closer terms with Ana's legendary brother than would have happened in normal circumstances. She had no doubt at all that the Conde de Pontalegre was not a man in the habit of confiding family secrets to strangers at his gate.

CHAPTER THREE

BY MORNING, however, the sleep which finally overtook Catherine had put everything back into perspective. She decided that her reaction to Eduardo Barroso was, if not a complete figment of her imagination, a lot to do with emotions disturbed by the sad little story he'd told her. In the bright light of day it was easy to relegate Eduardo to the slot where he belonged. A place marked 'Ana's brother', and nothing more. It was no part of her plan to make a fool of herself over a man she'd never see again in her life once Ana's wedding was over.

Dressed in the silk shirt of the night before, but with white jersey jogging pants in place of the skirt, she wove her hair into a loose braid and went down to the *sala* to find Eduardo, who was dressed in a blue polo shirt and sailcloth trousers, seated alone at a table set for two, with no sign of Ana. His eyes lit with the now familiar smile as he leapt to his feet to greet her. And that was that. All Catherine's theories about slots and common sense flew straight out of the veranda doors standing open to the morning sunshine.

'*Bom dia!*' He held out a chair for her. 'You slept well, Catherine?'

'Good morning.' She shook out a starched napkin, hoping her smile was on straight. 'I slept very well until the church bells woke me.'

'Ah! They are so much part of life here, we do not notice them.'

40

'I prefer their chimes to my alarm clock,' she assured him. 'Is Ana still in bed?'

'We went to early mass, then I advised her to return to bed for a while to avoid wearing herself out before her wedding day.' He smiled. 'Also, if I am truthful, I welcomed the opportunity of breakfasting alone with you.'

Catherine was so pleased by this piece of news that she had difficulty in keeping the pot steady as she poured coffee.

'I wished, you understand, to ask in private how you feel after the revelations of yesterday,' he went on, accepting the cup she offered.

The glow receded. 'Intrigued, but no longer haunted.' Catherine smiled cheerfully. 'My resemblance to your Isabel is just one of those extraordinary coincidences that happen in life. Isn't everyone supposed to have a double somewhere?'

He said nothing for a moment, scrutinising her face feature by feature as though still doubting the evidence of his own eyes. 'You must be right, of course. I have convinced myself overnight that I was mistaken. That you could not look so much like Isabel. Yet here and now, in the bright light of morning, the resemblance is still there.'

She frowned. 'Nevertheless, I hope you won't be offended if I ask you to think of me as plain Catherine Ward from now on, not some weird incarnation of your dead cousin.'

Eduardo's eyes narrowed to a cold glitter. '*Pois é.* It is not my habit to talk of Isabel at all. I deeply regret the necessity for burdening you with her story.'

Which puts *me* in my place, thought Catherine. 'Then let's forget it shall we? Isn't it a lovely day?'

'Ah, yes!' He looked amused. 'You English like to discuss the weather.'

'You take yours for granted,' she retorted, buttering one of Fernanda's rolls.

'Would you care for a cooked breakfast, English style? You have only to say the word.'

Catherine shook her head, eyeing the delicacies on offer, which included a dish of thinly sliced ham, fruit, toast, preserves and a basket of sweet as well as crusty rolls. 'Thank you, but I think there's more than enough here. Normally I don't eat breakfast at all.'

'You should. It is good to start the day with a meal.'

'So my mother keeps saying.' Catherine shrugged, smiling. 'Perhaps if I started every day in a place like this, looking out over that view outside, I *would* eat breakfast, just for the sheer pleasure of sitting here.'

'I feel this also,' he said smoothly. 'But not merely for the view, which I am accustomed to from birth. For me the pleasure comes from such charming company.'

'Not because I'm the spitting image of your Isabel?'

Eduardo's face emptied of expression. 'I thought we were to forget Isabel. But since you ask—no. It is not that. The resemblance is strong, *sem duvida*, but there are subtle differences. Your features are like hers, as though some master hand had created them with straight brush strokes. But your face is more resolute, Catherine. Isabel lacked such strength, also the sensual curve to your lower lip——'

Catherine's face burned. 'Please! You're embarrassing me.'

'*Perdõe-me*. It was not my intention.' He changed the subject smoothly, asking her what she would like to do once Ana joined them. 'Perhaps you would like to explore Pontalegre? I must spend a little time at Casa das Camelias with Elsa, the housekeeper, to make sure all is well with the current guests, but afterwards I will take you and Ana to lunch at one of the restaurants. If you wish,' he added punctiliously.

'I'd like that very much. But please don't feel you must. I could easily drive Ana to Pontalegre myself and let you get on with your day. If you wish,' she echoed, smiling a little.

Eduardo held out his cup for more coffee. 'Today is Sunday. Even one such as I must relax a little. Yesterday I worked like a dog in the *campo* until you arrived. Last night I was immersed in litigation problems until the small hours. Besides, your stay with us is so regrettably brief, I demand a *little* of your time, Catherine.'

'Demand?'

'Sometimes my English fails me.' He smiled, his eyes glinting. 'What would you prefer? Crave? Deserve? Desire?'

Catherine eyed him suspiciously. 'You're teasing me. How about plain "want"?'

'*Perfeito*,' he said softly, the gleam in his eyes so pronounced that Catherine looked away quickly.

'What time will Ana be up?'

'*Quem sabe*?' He shrugged. 'Until she appears perhaps you would care to see the rest of the house?'

The rooms still unexplored were all on the floor below. Eduardo showed Catherine how the space once used for wine storage had been utilised for the bedrooms occupied by himself and Ana, a large dining-room furnished in grand baronial style, with dark curved furniture and more armorial hangings, and next to the kitchen, where they found Fernanda listening to the radio while she prepared vegetables. She gave Catherine a warm greeting as she showed off her cheerful domain, which was tiled throughout in the familiar blue and white and yellow, with strings of onions and garlic suspended from the beams of the ceiling, along with bunches of herbs and drying grapes.

After telling Fernanda that they would be out to lunch, Eduardo escorted Catherine upstairs, frowning when she declared her intention of tidying her room.

'Fernanda can do that,' he objected.

'But she doesn't have to. I'm perfectly capable of making a bed!'

'I am sure you are capable of many things, Catherine.' He smiled very deliberately into her eyes, gave his now familiar bow, then watched her out of sight as she ran up the tower stairs.

Catherine was very thoughtful as she made her bed and straightened the room, wondering if she'd been wise to accept Ana's invitation after all. The Quinta das Lagoas was a beautiful house, and Ana's pleasure in her company was so obvious that she was glad to be here, of course. But it wouldn't do to let herself get too friendly with Ana's brother. She'd pictured him as middle-aged and married by now. But since he was neither of those things, and quite the most attractive man she'd met in her entire life, the wise course was to keep a very cool head in his vicinity. One disastrous love-affair was enough for anyone.

Catherine closed a mental door on her qualms as she joined Ana and Eduardo on the trip to Pontalegre, which she adored on sight. It was a small, charming little town of elegant old houses with weathered cin-

namon roofs, some of the buildings on the south side
of the river, but the main part rising steeply on the
north bank, the two halves linked by the symmetrical
stone arches of a bridge originally built by the
Romans. The river, Eduardo explained, had silted up
over the centuries, slowing the current and causing
the riverbed to widen, so that the bridge had to be
lengthened during the Middle Ages. Now there was a
wide, sandy beach either side of the river, and a
modern concrete bridge downstream from the town
for traffic, leaving the ancient one to pedestrians.

'And tomorrow,' said Ana, as Eduardo drove them
through narrow streets thronged with strolling Sunday
crowds, 'you will not see the shores of the river for
stalls and awnings. There is a *feira*—a fair—here every
fortnight, one of the biggest in the country.'

Eduardo nodded in agreement. 'Vendors bring their
wares from every part of the region, as they have since
the thirteenth century—everything from cattle to embroidered tablecloths.'

'Marvellous! A cow might present difficulties, but
my mother would love some embroidery——'
Catherine gave a gasp as Eduardo nonchalantly turned
the car up a cobbled street which at first sight seemed
vertical.

'Relax!' he said, with a sidelong grin at her petrified
face, which only relaxed when they reached the top,
where the road widened out into a small cobbled
square dominated by a great oblong of a house. One
balconied façade stood flush to the street, and the rest
of the building hid behind granite garden walls. The
architecture was typical seventeenth-century
Portuguese, Eduardo informed her. The lower walls
were blank except for tiny windows flanking the main

entrance door, while the upper floor sported a symmetrical row of french windows opening on to a wrought-iron balcony which girdled the house like a black lace sash.

'Welcome to Casa das Camelias,' said Eduardo with ceremony. He ushered Catherine into a great shadowy entance hall to the accompaniment of a great iron bell which clanged to announce their arrival. She shivered a little, cold from great granite flags striking through her sandals as Ana and Eduardo conducted her through an arched doorway and up a pair of stone staircases leading to the upper floor of the house.

'We live to the *esquerda*,' explained Ana, waving a hand to a pair of double doors which led through to a corridor on the left. 'The bedrooms for the visitors are to the right.'

This house silenced Catherine in a way the Quinta had failed to do. She looked in awe at the rifles and muskets mounted above shields and helmets on the walls, the piles of ancient cannon-balls in the corners on the landing. There were the familiar dark hangings everywhere embroidered with the same armorial bearings, and the rooms which interlinked by means of a series of double doors were filled with antique furniture and *objets d'art*, the library lined from floor to ceiling with leather-bound books of very obvious antiquity and value.

'This was my mother's favourite room,' said Ana. 'While Papae worked at his desk Mamae would sit here on the sofa with her embroidery.' She waved a hand at the hangings on the doors. 'These are all her work, those at the Quinta also.'

'Your mother was a very gifted lady!'

Eduardo nodded gravely. '*E verdade*. Come. Let us drink coffee with Elsa in our little private *sala*— which is very different from all this faded grandeur, you will find.'

Elsa was a stout, smiling woman in a black dress who ran the Casa das Camelias with the aid of two young girls from the town. Unlike Fernanda, Elsa had not had the privilege of Laura Dent's tuition. Nevertheless her English, though eccentric, was still sufficient to convey her delight at meeting Ana's college friend from England as she served them with coffee in the reassuringly cosy little *sala*, where glass doors stood open to give a tantalising view of the garden sequestered behind its high, concealing walls.

'You shall see the garden later,' promised Ana, presiding over the coffee tray. 'What do you think of Casa das Camelias?'

Eduardo's eyes were searching as Catherine tried to frame a reply. 'You do not like it?'

'Of course I do. How could I help it? But I prefer the Quinta,' she confessed. 'This one is very beautiful, of course, but rather more like a museum—less like a home.'

'It is home to us,' said Ana simply.

Catherine, well aware of this, smiled crookedly. 'You must have found life in Putney pretty strange, squashed into a tiny house with four other girls, Ana!'

'I was very fond of Putney.' Ana cast a roguish grin at her brother. 'There was no one there to order me about, remember!'

'You'll soon have Carlos to do that,' Eduardo reminded her.

'Just let him try!' Ana jumped up. 'I must give Elsa some messages from Fernanda. *Com licenca*,

Catherine.' She hurried off to the adjoining kitchen, leaving a rather strained silence behind her.

'I am sorry you do not care for Casa das Camelias,' remarked Eduardo at last.

Catherine met his eyes, startled. 'That's not true. It's a beautiful house.'

'It is also a burden,' he said heavily. 'Sometimes I wish I had sold it after Pedro died, as I was urged.'

By the brilliantly clever Antonia, no doubt, thought Catherine.

'But I could not,' he went on. 'It has been in my family for two hundred years. It would have broken my sisters' hearts. I was forced to take the only way out. I asked for government assistance.'

'Do you regret giving up your legal career?'

He shrugged. 'It is pointless to regret that which cannot be changed.'

Catherine's eyes shone with such sympathy that his expression altered, his eyes narrowing to a dark, intent gleam.

'What is it?' she asked quickly.

'Forgive me. It is just that you are so——'

'Like Isabel!' Catherine glared at him, and he smiled, the look in his eyes sending her blood racing through her veins.

He rose slowly to his feet, his eyes still locked with hers as he came to sit beside her on the worn brocade sofa. 'I was merely about to say that you are so very beautiful. *You*,' he repeated with emphasis. 'Miss Catherine Ward from England, of whom I had heard much, but had never met before yesterday. Which astonishes me, because I feel I know you well already.'

She retreated along the sofa a little. 'Only because of Isabel,' she muttered uncomfortably.

'Let us forget Isabel.' He captured her hand and raised it to his lips, but she snatched it away and jumped up to cross over to the window.

'I wish I could,' she said passionately, keeping her back turned.

She heard Eduardo get up, every nerve in her body quivering as he moved to stand close behind her, so close that she could feel the warmth of him through the thin silk of her shirt, feel his breath warm on the back of her neck. Catherine stood motionless, heart pounding, certain he meant to take her in his arms. Instead Eduardo flung away with a muffled curse a split second before Ana came running into the room to say that Elsa wouldn't hear of them having a restaurant lunch and insisted on providing a light meal, which would be ready in an hour.

'In the meantime,' proposed Ana, 'let us show you our town.'

'Does the idea please you, Catherine?' asked Eduardo.

'Very much,' she assured him, hoping her smile masked her mortifyingly bitter disappointment at the interruption.

When they set out on foot to descend through the narrow cobbled streets Catherine kept close to Ana, with the firm intention of distancing herself from Eduardo as much as possible, short of looking obvious. Eduardo, a narrowed glance in her direction telling her that he knew exactly what she was about, pointed out the various churches and landmarks, the tower which had once housed the town gaol, and which was currently being transformed into a new records library. Catherine listened, fascinated, her wariness vanished as Eduardo explained that the granite blocks used in the restoration were still hammered out by hand, just as they had been for centuries.

'But isn't that extraordinarily time-consuming?'

Ana laughed. 'We take a different view of time here, *querida*.'

It was very pleasant to walk along the avenue of plane trees lining the river bank. Catherine felt surprised to feel so utterly at home as they mingled with the crowds who emerged from the various churches to stroll along in the sunshine on the way home, some of them making for restaurants to eat a family lunch, others to drink coffee in the numerous little bars and cafés dotted all over town.

'Shall we have a drink in the *praca*?' asked Eduardo, as they retraced their footsteps, but Ana shook her head firmly.

'Elsa will have lunch ready—also we must not be late back at the Quinta because Carlos dines with us tonight. He is looking forward to meeting Catherine.'

Eduardo flicked a teasing finger at her cheek. 'Perhaps he will love you no longer once he lays eyes on your beautiful friend!'

'It is possible, *sem duvida*,' Ana agreed, unruffled.

'I was only teasing, *carinha*,' he assured her. 'Come, then, *meninas*, let us go back to the house. I have no wish to displease Elsa—particularly,' he added darkly, 'now I am deserted, and must run the business alone. I shall be doubly dependent on both Elsa and Fernanda.'

'Have you had no success at all with finding a replacement for Ana?' enquired Catherine.

'None,' said Ana, giggling. 'He is very hard to please. Which is why he is *solteiro* still. No bride has ever been found who is perfect enough for him.'

Eduardo threw his sister a repressive look as they climbed up the steep street to the Casa das Camelias. 'I have never had time to find a wife,' he said shortly. 'Not, I am sure, that our guest is interested in so boring a subject.'

Wrong, thought Catherine as she followed Ana into the house. The topic interested her far more than it should.

The simple lunch was eaten in the formality of a dining-room with a gleaming floor of grey and rose granite.

'Will your wedding breakfast be served here?' asked Catherine.

'Oh, no!' Ana laughed. 'There are too many guests for that. The meal will be what you call a buffet. It will be served outside in the courtyard, which is floodlit at night, and after the meal we shall dance!'

'Ana's wedding, as you can see,' remarked Eduardo drily, 'is not likely to resemble any other in your experience, Catherine.'

'I'm looking forward to it immensely. By the way, Eduardo,' said Catherine curiously, 'will you be in Minhota costume too?'

He grimaced. '*Não, senhora*! I refuse to make a fool of myself in fancy dress even for my darling little sister. Carlos, of course,' he added sardonically, 'has surrendered to Ana's pleading, the besotted young fool. I have warned that he must be stricter with her once they are married or *sem duvida* his life will be hell!'

While Eduardo consulted with Elsa after lunch Ana took Catherine outside to show her the garden. A colonnade ran along the side of the house giving on to the courtyard where the reception would take place.

The pillars, which bore the original iron rings once used to tether horses, were festooned with creeper which blazed red against the white walls of the house in the bright afternoon sunshine. Catherine, camera at the ready, was allowed only two shots of the scene before Ana hurried her to a flight of stone steps ascending from a corner of the courtyard to the garden itself, most of which was level with the upper floor of the house.

Catherine exclaimed with delight at the sight of four great camellia trees planted in proximity to provide a canopy of shade for garden chairs grouped near a small swimming-pool. The water glinted green in the afternoon sunlight, watched over by two cheerful little stone monks on granite pillars among a profusion of ferns and the blue spherical heads of tall agapanthus. Along the ivy-clad garden wall behind them a row of sweet chestnuts shed their furry-coated fruit from time to time on the grass, the soft thump clearly audible in the Sunday hush. Catherine darted about, taking shots from every possible angle, including the knot garden beyond, until Ana called a halt.

'It is time to interrupt Eduardo,' she said, looking at her watch. 'We must leave immediately to give me time to make myself beautiful for Carlos when we return to the Quinta.'

Catherine chuckled as they went back into the cool, shadowy house. 'You don't need hours for that, Ana—in fact you look quite lovely just the way you are!'

To her surprise Ana turned a very serious look on her as they climbed the stone staircase to the upper floor. 'It is only for a little while that I shall have time to do this, Catherine. While I am still *solteira*. Once

I marry Carlos life, I know well, will change. But for just these last few days before the *nupcial* I wish to spend every moment possible on my looks. I want my *noivo* more impatient to possess me every time we meet, so that when we come together as man and wife at last it will be perfection.'

Catherine paused at the first landing, her eyes troubled. 'Oh, Ana, don't expect too much. Not—not the first time.'

Ana slid her arms round Catherine's waist and hugged her hard. 'For me it will be perfect. For you, with a lover like your Dan,' she added with startling candour, 'I knew well it could not have been, *querida*. But he was just a selfish boy, unworthy to kiss your feet. My Carlos is a man, and different.'

Catherine found Ana's words hard to put from her mind. She was so quiet on the way back to the Quinta that Eduardo eyed her narrowly from time to time as he drove, and eventually asked if she was feeling unwell. Assuring him she was fine, she began to talk about the garden at Casa das Camelias with an animation that he listened to politely for a while before asking again if there was something wrong. She glanced over at Ana, who was stretched out on the back seat, sound asleep.

'It's just that I can't help worrying for Ana,' she said in an undertone.

'Because she expects to be happy ever after, as they say in your fairy-tales?' Eduardo smiled reassuringly. 'Do not disturb yourself, Catherine. When you meet him you will see she has chosen the right man in Carlos.'

'I'm glad.' Catherine stared fixedly at her clasped hands. 'I just hope he appreciates how she feels.'

'Her aim for perfection, you mean?'

She stared at him, appalled. 'You heard us talking on the stairs?'

He looked a trifle discomfited. 'Yes. It was not my intention to—to eavesdrop?'

She turned away sharply, her face flaming.

'Nevertheless sound carries in the hall of Casa das Camelias. I could not help hearing Ana's supreme faith in the wonder of her wedding night.' Eduardo gave her an unsettling sidelong glance. 'Also I heard her remarks about your *noivo*—and the nature of your relationship. Catherine, do not feel ashamed——'

'Ashamed!' Catherine rounded on him with a fierce whisper, her eyes blazing with resentment. 'I'm not in the least ashamed of my relationship with Dan—which, incidentally, is nothing to do with you.'

'Forgive me, Catherine,' he said in a rapid undertone. 'I had no wish to give offence. Remember that I have little practice in speaking your language these days. I do not choose the right words always. I am sorry.'

Catherine simmered in silence for a while, furious with herself for letting Eduardo Barroso get under her skin so easily. 'So am I for being so rude,' she said stiffly at first, forcing a smile. 'You know, I feel quite tired. It must be this wonderful air of yours. Perhaps I'll have a rest before dinner.'

Eduardo's face set into a polite mask as he turned in through the arch at Quinta das Lagoas. '*Pois é*. You are free to do as you wish, always, Catherine. We shall not dine until eight.'

'*Chegamos*?' asked a sleepy voice from the back as Eduardo turned the car through the archway. 'We have arrived?'

CHAPTER FOUR

CATHERINE, more put out by the small scene with Eduardo than she would have believed possible, fully expected to pass the time before dinner with one of the paperback novels bought at the airport. Instead the overdose of emotional strain sent her straight to sleep the moment she flung herself down on the bed. She woke in darkness, disorientated and yawning, to urgent tapping on the bedroom door.

'Catherine!' called Ana. 'Are you all right?'

'Come in,' said Catherine sleepily. She fumbled with the bedside lamp, then shot upright in horror. 'Oh, glory—look at the time!'

'I have been up before,' said Ana, coming into the room. 'But when I saw no light I thought you must be asleep. Eduardo said not to disturb you because you were tired.' She sat down on the edge of the bed, touching a hand to Catherine's flushed cheek. 'If you are *very* tired you could have a tray in bed, *querida*.'

For a moment Catherine was tempted. The prospect of avoiding Eduardo Barroso for the evening was alluring. But cowardly. She shook her head, sliding out of bed. 'Of course not, Ana—I'm dying to meet this bridegroom of yours, silly!' She eyed the other girl's jade silk dress with respect. 'You look gorgeous. Just give me twenty minutes. I don't say I'll look as stunning as you, but I promise not to let the side down, Senhorita Barroso.'

'*Bobagem*!' said Ana, hugging her. 'Take as much time as you wish. We shall be in the *sala*. I have bullied Fernanda to serve dinner there again instead of in state downstairs. See you later—*até já*!'

Catherine took two minutes to stand under a bracingly cool shower, then spent another five on half drying her hair. She dressed swiftly in an apricot linen skirt and plain white silk T-shirt, then spent several more minutes on her hair, brushing it up and away from her face to coil it smoothly on the crown of her head. To complement the severity of the style she emphasised her eyes more heavily than usual, sprayed herself sparingly with perfume, then just as a clock struck eight somewhere in the depths of the house she put on the matching apricot jacket, slid her feet into fawn linen pumps, attached a cascade of amber drops to each ear and took a deep breath to compose herself. Right, Catherine, she told herself. Best foot forward.

Shyness was something new to Catherine. When she reached the hall she stood still at the foot of the stairs, suddenly paralysed with it, yearning to run back to her room and plead weariness after all rather than come face to face with Eduardo Barroso again. Then she caught her breath, rooted to the spot, as her host, dauntingly elegant in a formal dark suit, appeared through the double doors leading from the *sala*. He closed them very quietly behind him, gazing across the room at her in unnerving silence for an interval before crossing the stone-flagged floor to join her.

Catherine smiled at him uneasily. 'Good evening.'

'*Boa tarde*, Catherine,' he said at last, and threw out his hands in a gesture of disbelief. 'I am amazed.'

'Amazed?'

'Ana said you were still sleeping when she went to your room half an hour ago.'

'I was.'

'And yet here you are. Not only punctual, but a vision to dazzle the eyes.'

Catherine relaxed, feeling rather better. 'The cabin I shared on the cruise liner was so small, my companion and I had to take turns at getting ready. We got used to dressing at top speed.'

'I am certain Carlos would be grateful if you instructed Ana in such an art!' He smiled. 'Otherwise much of his life will be spent pacing the floor like a caged lion, as he has this evening.'

'But Ana was ready ages ago!' she said, laughing.

Eduardo shrugged. 'After talking to you she returned to her room to rearrange her hair. Carlos has passed the time since his arrival striving to make intelligent conversation with me while consulting his watch at every possible moment. Now Ana has finally joined him at last I took pity on him and came in here to wait for you to come down. I confess I did not expect you for some time yet.'

'Now I am here shouldn't we join them?'

'In a little while. Let them have their moment together.' His eyes met hers with sudden significance. 'Besides, I am grateful for this unexpected privacy. I wish to know if I am forgiven.'

She tensed. 'Forgiven?'

'I think you know why, Catherine. I should not have told you I overheard such a private conversation between you and Ana. You were embarrassed and angry, *naturalmente*. I apologise.'

'I wasn't angry because you overheard! It was your implication that I had something to be ashamed of which made my blood boil.'

He moved closer. 'I know this.' His eyes narrowed to a dark, intent glitter. 'I expressed myself badly because what I heard——' He shrugged, a look of self-derision on his aquiline face. 'You may laugh if you wish, but when I learned you and this—this man of yours were lovers I felt jealous.'

Catherine stared at him blankly. 'You can't be serious!'

'Why not?'

'We've only just met.'

'I find it difficult to remember this.'

'Because I look like Isabel!'

'No! I no longer think of her when I see you. For Isabel I had dreams—adolescent worship.' He took her hand, looking deep into her eyes. 'Will I offend you, Catherine, if I say that for you my feelings are very much those of a man for a woman?'

They gazed at each other in silence, Catherine trying to hide her reaction to the clasp of his fingers, which tightened as his eyes narrowed to a molten gleam, a vein throbbing at the corner of his mouth.

Suddenly she jerked her hand away. 'This is a mistake,' she informed him coldly. 'Your mistake. What you overheard misled you. I'm not in the market for—for what you seem to have in mind.'

Eduardo's eyes flashed angrily. 'How can you know what I have in mind?'

'The same as most men, I imagine!'

'Your experience of my sex has not been happy, *é verdade*!' His mouth took on a sardonic curve. 'You

may sleep untroubled in your bed, I swear, Catherine.
As a guest under my roof you have nothing to fear.'

She climbed down a little. 'Thank you. I'm
relieved.'

'But I would lie if I denied that my blood leaps
every time I look at you. Yet my response, you understand, is not only to your beauty but to your intelligence—a quality I much admire in a woman. Also,
it is a long time since I was a hot-headed student blind
to everything but my own desires.' He smiled
crookedly. 'Such a long speech! I have bored you.'

'No!' she said quickly. 'I jumped to the wrong conclusion. I'm sorry. And my sincere thanks for the
compliment. About the intelligence, I mean. Most
men just look at the cover and don't bother about
the book inside.'

Eduardo put her hard-won composure at risk by
raising her hand to his lips before escorting her across
the room. When he turned the great iron knob on the
door to the *sala* he smiled at Catherine wickedly as
he gave it an emphatic warning rattle before ushering
her through to join the pair who had quite obviously
only just sprung apart at the interruption.

Ana, flushed and very slightly dishevelled, came
running to take Catherine's hand. 'Let me present you
to Carlos,' she said breathlessly.

The slim young man who advanced towards
Catherine with outstretched hand was much darker
than the Barrosos, with black curling hair and a smile
which shone white in his olive-skinned face, which
was so strong-featured and open that all Catherine's
fears for Ana evaporated as Carlos da Cunha greeted
her in heavily accented English, his smile warm as he

told Catherine how enchanted he was to meet Ana's beautiful friend at last.

'Eduardo said that perhaps once you set eyes on Catherine you would not want me any more,' Ana informed him.

Carlos turned to her with mock-resignation, his eyes dancing. 'It is a possibility, *de certeza*,' he agreed. 'Alas, since all is arranged, perhaps it is best we proceed with the *casamento*.'

'You are supposed to say no one is more beautiful than me!' she said, laughing.

'*Porquê?* You know that for me this is the truth,' he said simply, then bowed in Catherine's direction. 'If your friend will forgive me.'

'I do indeed.' Catherine smiled warmly, much taken with the natural charm of Ana's fiancé. She felt more than a little wistful at the sight of the two young lovers together at first, but as the evening progressed realised she was enjoying herself enormously, aware that her rise in spirits owed much to the interlude with Eduardo beforehand.

The conversation was fast and furious, with spasmodic lapses into his own tongue by Carlos when he needed Ana as an interpreter, something which added to the fun considerably, since the naughty Ana tended to give very free translations, Eduardo being in no mood for reprimand for once.

'I have given up,' he informed Carlos, grinning. 'Soon she will be your responsibility, *gracas a Deus*.'

Since this fate was obviously the one her future husband desired more than anything in the world Ana failed to rise to Eduardo's teasing.

'You will miss me when you are left alone with the office work,' she assured her brother tartly.

He sighed, shrugging. '*Quem sabe*? Perhaps someone suitable will apply for the post before the problem finally arises.'

'He is waiting for Miss Perfect,' giggled Ana, as they left the table.

Carlos, intrigued to hear how Catherine had spent her time since college, was obviously puzzled that a girl would prefer to sell clothes to cruising holiday-makers rather than seek a post more in keeping with her business training. Over some very special port Eduardo produced to mark the occasion, Catherine gave her usual explanation about wanting to see something of the world before settling down.

'Also, Catherine wished to get over an unhappy love-affair,' Ana informed him, her face suddenly scarlet as she met her brother's disapproving frown. 'I am sorry, *querida*,' she said in remorse, taking Catherine's hand. 'I have the big mouth, *não é*?'

'No, love,' said Catherine lightly. 'It's the truth, after all. And as a cure the travelling was very effective. I worked hard, met some interesting people, and in between times visited a lot of far-away places I would never have seen otherwise.'

'Where did you go, Catherine?' asked Carlos quickly, eager to divert Eduardo's displeasure from Ana.

'Oh, most of the Mediterranean ports, the Caribbean—the popular places. I never got to the Far East, unfortunately.'

In response to Ana's urging Catherine described her rather uneventful social life afloat. Her meals had been eaten mainly in a ward-room with some of the junior officers, and sometimes there were parties with the crew in the band-room behind the stage in the main entertainment lounge.

'And very occasionally,' she added, 'I was invited to a meal in one of the passenger dining-rooms.'

'By a male passenger, of course!' said Ana.

Conscious of Eduardo, silent but intent at her side on the sofa, Catherine nodded matter-of-factly.

Ana looked envious. 'It sounds exciting.' She grinned mischievously at Catherine. 'Did you ever have problems afterwards? When your dinner partner escorted to your cabin?'

'*Querida*!' remonstrated Carlos. 'You must not ask such things.'

Catherine smiled. 'I don't mind. Problems never arose because I always made it clear my company at dinner was all the gentleman could expect. Now,' she added briskly, 'enough about me. Tell me about your plans for developing your home for tourism, Carlos.'

Since this was a subject dear to his heart Carlos went into great detail, pressing Catherine to return to Portugal on holiday to see for herself once he and Ana were installed in the Quinta da Floresta. 'I know of your kindness to Ana in her time of sorrow,' he said gently. 'Our home is yours always, whenever you wish.'

Catherine, deeply touched, promised to visit them some day. 'I shall be glad of a place to run to, I expect, once I'm working ashore.'

'Has a business career always been your goal?' asked Eduardo.

'More or less.'

'You have no man in your life now?' asked Carlos, interested.

'No.' Catherine shrugged. 'I'm not as lucky as Ana. I'm still waiting for Mr Right.'

When Carlos looked blank Ana laughed. She jumped up, holding out her hand to him. 'Come, *meu amor*. I shall explain while I walk you to your car.'

The young man's alacrity was so blatant that Catherine bit back a chuckle as she met Eduardo's amused eyes. Carlos said his goodnights eagerly, thanked Eduardo for the evening, then kissed Catherine's hand.

Eduardo looked at his watch. 'Since it is so near your wedding, Ana, I grant you a few minutes extra to say goodnight.'

Ana made a swift, mocking obeisance. '*Que irmão bondoso*! My brother is *so* kind,' she informed Catherine, casting her eyes heavenwards. 'Do *you* think I need his permission to bid my *noivo* goodnight?'

'You do if it takes half the night to do so,' retorted Eduardo, and waved her away. 'Go. Before I regret such generosity. May I give you another drink, Catherine?' he added, as the lovers fled joyfully away.

'No more wine, thank you. A tonic water perhaps?'

'*Pois é*.' He busied himself at a side-table, returning with an ice-filled glass of tonic and a modest whisky for himself. 'I shall allow myself the luxury of tasting your gift, Catherine. *Saúde*!'

She returned the toast, wishing Ana would hurry up as Eduardo seated himself in his former place beside her on the sofa. Now they were alone the atmosphere was subtly different, tinged with a slight tension left over from the encounter in the hall before dinner. Catherine sat very still, her eyes straight ahead. But just within her line of vision she could see

Eduardo's hand curled round his glass, fine hairs dark against the bronzed skin below his white shirt cuff, a crested gold cuff-link catching a gleam of light from the lamp at his elbow. And suddenly she was so overwhelmingly conscious of his nearness that her hand shook, rattling the ice cubes in her glass.

'Catherine.'

'Yes?' She put the traitorous glass down without looking at him.

'Something troubles you? You wish me to leave you alone to wait for Ana?'

'Of course not.'

'Then look at me.'

At the unemphatic note of command in his voice Catherine turned her head, her pulse quickening as she met the caressing look in his eyes. He consulted his watch, a smile playing at the corners of his mouth.

'It is now almost thirty-two hours since we met, Catherine. Soon we shall be able to describe ourselves as old friends.'

She smiled wryly. 'No one else would!'

'You care for the opinion of others?'

'Of course. People who matter to me, anyway.'

'Is there someone back in England who matters in this way?' he asked carefully, staring into his glass.

'My mother, quite a lot of friends.'

'But no lover?'

Catherine drank some of her tonic. 'Eduardo, let's get something straight. Your English is extremely good. Your Dona Laura would be proud of you. But I'm not sure what you mean by "lover". It's a word I've never had occasion to use. It implies some relationship a whole lot closer than anything I've ever had with a man.'

Eduardo frowned, his slim brows drawn together in a straight line. 'Then what was this—this Dan I heard about?' He paused. 'Or perhaps you think I trespass. That this is also nothing to do with me?'

Catherine eyed him contemplatively. 'I won't say that again, I promise. But what you don't understand is that Dan was merely a boyfriend. That's all. Our relationship was just a college romance, only I was too inexperienced to realise it at the time.'

Eduardo moved closer and took her hand. 'Then why were you so unhappy that you needed to travel the world to get over it?'

She looked him in the eye. 'Ah, but at the time I thought it was more important. Not that my heart was dented too badly, as it happened. It was my pride which suffered the most damage.' She withdrew her hand as quick footsteps on the veranda heralded Ana's arrival. Eduardo rose to his feet, eyeing his flushed sister with a quizzical gleam in his eye.

'So. You have torn yourself away at last.'

'I am sure you did not miss me with Catherine to keep you company,' said Ana pertly, smoothing her hair. 'And soon, *querido irmão*, you need worry about me no longer. I shall be Senhora da Cunha, *se Deus quizer*.'

'I sincerely hope God does so will it,' said Eduardo with mock piety. 'Poor Carlos.'

'Poor Carlos *nada*!' she retorted, and danced round the room, her skirt fluttering to the danger of various ornaments dotted round on small tables. 'Lucky Carlos!' She stopped dead in the middle of the room, her eyes suddenly serious in her vivid face. 'And lucky Ana Maria also. He will be a very good husband.'

'I know it,' said Eduardo drily. 'Otherwise I would not permit you to marry him. Come here.' He embraced her very tenderly. 'And you will make him a good wife, *carinha*. Now. Would you like something to drink?'

'*Não, obrigado*, Eduardo.' Ana yawned suddenly, apologetic as she came to kiss Catherine's cheek. 'Forgive me, *querida*. I am so sleepy suddenly. Will you think me rude if I go to bed?' She cast a mischievous glance at her brother. 'I am sure Eduardo is desolated to have me leave, but perhaps you will take pity on his loneliness.'

Catherine patted her cheek, ignoring the last bit. 'Of course you're not rude—besides, I'm off to bed myself in a minute.'

'After that long sleep this afternoon?' Ana shook her head. 'I think she should stay up for a while. You agree, Eduardo?'

'Allow your guest to do as she wishes,' he said sternly. 'Go to bed, Ana. *Boa noite.*'

Catherine finished her drink quickly once Ana had trailed, yawning, from the room. 'I should be going to bed too.'

'Are you tired?'

'Not very,' she admitted. 'But I brought several books with me. If I can't get to sleep I'll read. Besides, you must be tired, even if I'm not.'

Eduardo shook his head. When she refused his offer of another drink he poured himself a sparing amount of whisky, then sat in a chair opposite Catherine. 'It is not yet eleven-thirty. I rarely go to bed before midnight, often much later. Will you not grant me the pleasure of your company for a few short minutes longer, while I savour this excellent whisky?'

Something in his tone would have made it impossible for Catherine to refuse even if she'd had any desire to. There was nothing she wanted more than to stay here in this beautiful room, in the company of this cultured, handsome man who made it gratifyingly plain that he was attracted to her. Besides, she thought bleakly, her stay here would be short. And once she left Quinta das Lagoas it was highly unlikely she'd meet a man like Eduardo Barroso again in her entire life.

'Since you have not fled, am I to understand that you will stay?' he asked softly, his eyes on her thoughtful face. 'Or does it trouble you to remain here alone with me?'

'No. It doesn't trouble me.' She smiled candidly. 'I'll be honest. I enjoy your company.'

His smile dazzled her. 'I rejoice to know you find my company as agreeable as I do yours, Catherine. But have no fear. I do not mistake your statement for permission to make love to you. Much as I long to do so.' He gave his slight, characteristic shrug. 'I say this, you understand, because I wish us to be frank with each other.'

Catherine nodded, feeling very much more relaxed. 'So do I. So I'll admit that the idea isn't exactly repugnant to me, either. No!' She held up a hand as he looked ready to spring from his chair. 'All I'm saying is that the attraction is completely mutual.'

Eduardo sat tense as a coiled spring, regarding her with a look which made her cheeks burn. 'You tell me this and expect me to keep the distance from you? I may not be a heedless youth any more, Catherine, but I am still a man!'

She sighed. 'I had noticed! But because you're a mature, *civilised* man, Eduardo Barroso, surely you can understand that for the short time I'm here it would be madness to get too involved.'

'It is too late for that,' he said with force. 'I think you know this very well. From the moment I first held you in my arms when you arrived there has been a bond between us.'

'Only because I look like Isabel Cardoso!'

Eduardo's eyes glittered with triumph. '*Não, senhora*! When I lifted you from the car you wore a scarf over your hair and dark glasses hid most of your face. My reaction was one of pure instinct—nothing to do with your looks, *carinha*.'

Catherine stared at his urgent face in silence for a moment. 'Is that true?'

'You doubt my word?' he demanded with hauteur.

'No, no.' She drew in a deep, unsteady breath, feeling distinctly shaken.

Eduardo rose and came to sit beside her, careful to leave distance between them on the sofa. 'This resemblance was a shock, *de certeza*. When I first saw your lovely face I could not believe my eyes. But Isabel, remember, was five years younger than you when she died. Her face lacked the qualities of strength and maturity which I so admire in yours. As I grow to know you better, each hour the resemblance fades.' With care, giving her time to draw away, he took her hand in his, his eyes compelling. 'Even after such a short time it is you alone I see, Catherine, not poor, tragic Isabel.'

Her eyes dropped to their linked hands. 'I'm glad. But it makes no difference. Once I leave here I'll never see you again. Bond or no bond——' She faltered as his grasp tightened.

'Why should we never meet again?' he demanded fiercely. 'Do you not wish to?'

Her head flew up. 'I live in England and your life is here. The arrangement doesn't exactly lend itself to casual meetings! I'll be busy with whatever job I find—and you with yours. So I think I'd better say goodnight.'

Appalled by a traitorous thickening in her throat, Catherine turned her head, biting down hard on her lower lip. Eduardo turned her face up to his, his eyes narrowing at the shine of tears in hers. With a stifled sound he caught her in his arms, kissing her trembling mouth, the first touch of his lips enough to melt away her iron resolve as though it had never been. His embrace, intended to comfort, altered dramatically as their bodies strained together. Eduardo's breathing accelerated, his mouth wild in its demand as his arms locked round her like a vice. Catherine uttered a stifled moan of surprise at the urgency which transmitted from his body to hers like a lighted fuse, streaking along her nerves, setting her alight with longing in a way which frightened her out of her wits.

'Eduardo—stop!' she cried frantically, and at once he raised his head, his eyes alight with triumph.

'You see!' he panted. 'You cannot deny this bond.'

'Bond?' She swallowed, shivering. 'Is that what it is?'

Eduardo's eyes burned into hers. 'What would you call it, *querida*?'

Catherine gazed back, ensnared. 'I don't know. I've never experienced anything remotely like that before.'

She felt him tense. 'Never?'

'No.'

'Not even——' He halted sharply, as though he couldn't bring himself to say the name.

'I said *never*,' she repeated, so emphatically that he bent his head and kissed her fiercely, sliding his hands into her hair until she couldn't have moved away a centimetre, even if she'd wanted to.

At last he raised his head to look down into eyes as dark now as his, the amber irises hidden by pupils dilated with desire—a fact he commented on with such male relish that her lashes came down like shutters to hide the evidence.

'Has no one told you before that your eyes look so when you love?' he asked huskily.

'No. And I wish you'd stop discussing my past love-life.' She tried to break free but he held her fast. 'I haven't asked a word about yours.'

'You may know everything about me—and my love-life—that you ask, *amada*,' he assured her, laughing. 'There is less to tell you than you imagine, I swear.'

'I don't think I want to know,' she said slowly, looking up into the intent dark eyes so close to hers. She pushed back a lock of straying hair. 'Besides——'

'Go on,' he commanded.

'This doesn't change anything, Eduardo. When I fly home next week——'

'Why must you go?'

'Because my airline ticket——'

'Buy another ticket.'

'No, I can't.'

'Why not?'

'A simple matter of economics. Money, Eduardo, money!'

'I will pay for it,' he said at once.

'No!' She put up a hand to touch his cheek. 'Look. Once Ana's married there's no reason for me to stay here. Your family would have a fit.'

He scowled. 'A fit?'

'I mean they'd be surprised, and I wouldn't blame them.'

'If I invite you to stay here as my guest my family would not question your presence,' he said loftily. 'They would not dare.'

'Possibly not. Nevertheless it's out of the question.'

His face hardened. 'You mean you do not wish to stay.'

Catherine sighed in despair. 'I do, I do. But I can't. So let's drop the subject.'

'Can you not be persuaded?' he asked softly, a light in his eye which set her heart hammering.

'Very probably.' She leapt to her feet. 'Nevertheless I'm not going to let you make love to me again.'

'Never?' He rose slowly to his feet with the grace and purpose of a tiger about to spring.

Catherine backed away.

'Tell me you do not wish me to and I shall not even try.' He caught her by the wrist. 'Well? *A verdade*, Catherine. The truth.'

When her pulse was throbbing like a wild thing against his fingers it seemed pointless to lie. 'All right! You win. I do want you to. But it makes no difference. Can't you see, Eduardo? I can't let you make love to me——'

He pulled her to him and held her close, pulling the pins from the knot so that he could bury his face in her tumbling hair. 'I have not even begun to make love to you, Catherine,' he said in a muffled voice. 'The kisses, the caresses, they were a mere *ideia*—a foretaste of the joy we could experience together.'

A cold shiver ran down her spine. 'Eduardo, don't! Two days ago we'd never met. And since Dan there's been no one. Not in that way. I promised myself I'd have to be very sure before——'

'Catherine, I am not demanding to be your lover.' His arms tightened. 'Though, *Deus me livre*, there is nothing I want more. At this moment I would give much to come with you to my old room in the tower and make love to you until dawn, but for many reasons this is not possible. You are Ana's friend, and my guest, under my protection.' He gave a short laugh. '*Deus*, I had not foreseen that it would be myself you must be protected from! But do not deny this magic between us. I feel it like a silken thread, binding us together. I do not care that we have known each other such a short time, Catherine. Surely we can be loving friends?'

She drew away gently, her eyes luminous as they met his. 'You mean a few kisses and embraces, with no harm done? That way lies temptation, and I'm afraid to get hurt again, Eduardo.'

'I will never hurt you, *querida*,' he said with such conviction that she smiled sadly.

'Not knowingly. But you probably will just the same. So no more interludes like this, please.'

He gazed at her, frustrated, a pulse throbbing at the corner of his mouth. 'Very well, Catherine. I have no choice but to obey.'

'Thank you.' With effort she managed a smile. 'Goodnight, Eduardo.'

'Stay a little longer,' he said abruptly. 'Do not leave me yet, *por favor*. I promise not to touch you if you will stay and talk for a while.' His eyes lit with sudden inspiration. 'Perhaps you would like some tea?'

CHAPTER FIVE

CATHERINE giggled, the sudden descent into the mundane snapping the tension between them. 'Now that's an offer I can't refuse! Where do I make it?'

His face relaxed. 'We shall go down to Fernanda's kitchen. Most of our guests in the tourist season are English. It is her habit to keep a tea-tray in readiness.'

They stole downstairs like conspirators, Eduardo pointing out the kettle and the jar which contained tea, but otherwise leaving the process in Catherine's hands.

'Have you ever made tea?' she asked, as she poured boiling water into the pot. 'Or cooked at all, if it comes to that?'

'As a student I sometimes made a simple meal, but alas never the tea. Does this banish me from your regard forever?'

Catherine shook her head as he took the tray from her to carry it upstairs. 'I could hardly expect the Conde de Pontalegre to be domesticated!'

'The title has been mine for only a very short time,' he reminded her as they reached the *sala*. 'I was plain Eduardo Barroso most of my life.'

'I wouldn't say plain, exactly!' Catherine looked at him searchingly as they resumed their places on the sofa. 'You must miss your former life.'

Eduardo nodded, confessing that, given the choice, he would prefer to pursue his legal career than manage the family properties. The death of his brother in a road accident had thrust Eduardo Barroso into the role of head of the family without warning, followed almost at once by the crushing blow of his mother's death. When the Condessa suffered a fatal heart attack at the news of Pedro's accident Eduardo was left with a double tragedy to cope with, forced to sublimate his own searing grief in his efforts to comfort his sisters and sort out their inheritance.

'I loved Pedro,' he said sombrely. 'But certain events shaped his life in a way which destroyed his interest in his inheritance. Fortunately I possess more aptitude for commerce. The government grant and the income from the tourists and the *rendeiros* secured the houses, *gracas a Deus*.'

Catherine poured herself a second cup of tea, frowning. 'But there's not much spare cash, I take it.'

'Not as much as I would wish.' Eduardo smiled wryly. 'Ana has come in for much criticism for her choice of a Minhota wedding, but she knows that a couturier dress and an expensive reception like Leonor's and Cristina's would cost a great deal more than the simple country wedding she has chosen.'

'I see,' said Catherine thoughtfully. Ana, as she knew, was far more astute than her carefree attitude led most people to believe. 'But, being Ana, she'll enjoy her wedding day to the full anyway. She always makes the very best of things. The only time I remember her utterly crushed was after——'

'After the accident,' he agreed sombrely. '*Coitada*. Her light was extinguished entirely for a while. Pedro's death was tragedy enough, but the loss of my mother was devastating. For all of us.' He took Catherine's hand. 'Without you to give comfort and support in so dark a time Ana would not be as she is today.'

'I didn't do very much, Eduardo. I was just there for her, that's all. A shoulder to cry on. I'm very, very fond of Ana. It wasn't difficult to give what comfort I could.'

'Could you be "fond" of me?' he asked abruptly.

Catherine's smile was wry. Fond seemed a lukewarm word in connection with Eduardo Barroso. 'Since we're to be friends, I suppose the answer must be yes.'

'You do not say this with conviction!'

'Because "fond" doesn't seem right.'

'My English is at fault again?'

She smiled. 'It isn't the word I'd choose, that's all.'

'What is the word?' he demanded.

'I'll let you know when I've thought of one. Now I really must go, Eduardo. It's very late.'

'I shall escort you to your room, Catherine.' He smiled into her wary eyes. 'Do not fear. I shall not come inside. But the Quinta is haunted, it is said. You might need me for protection from ghosts on the stairs.'

'Thanks a lot! You're just saying that so I'll plead with you to come with me.'

'If you wish to believe that, of course you may!'

Although she gave a stifled little laugh as they crossed the cavernous hall Catherine was glad when Eduardo took her hand in his. The dim lighting was no match for moonlight which struck through the deep window embrasures and cast strange shadows, investing the suit of armour with a spectral look of life. A cold tremor ran down her spine, strangely at odds with the heat flowing through her veins from their joined hands. They fell silent as they mounted the stairs, their footsteps growing slower and slower until they came to a halt at last on the small landing outside her bedroom door. Eduardo stood looking down at her, his face as stern as a piece of sculpture in the shaft of moonlight striking through the tower window.

'Catherine?'

'Yes?' she whispered.

'If you send me away without one kiss of goodnight I shall not sleep.'

Hypnotised by the glitter in his eyes, she moved the inch which separated them, holding up her face to his. As their lips met Eduardo's arms locked about her with a forceful tenderness which turned Catherine's bones to water. He drew her up on tiptoe, moulding her pliant body against his as they drowned together in the intensity of the kiss. At last, when neither could breathe, he tore his mouth away and pressed her face to his shoulder, his cheek against her hair. They stood in taut, throbbing silence until their pulses slowed and their breathing steadied, Eduardo holding her in an embrace of such ravishing security that Catherine felt cold when at last his arms reluctantly fell away.

'Will you sleep now?' she whispered.

'No, I will not!' he said with violence, then raised her hand to his parted lips, pressing a kiss into her palm. '*Boa noite*, Catherine.'

She swallowed hard, curling her hand shut. 'Goodnight, Eduardo.' She opened the door then turned to him with a rueful smile. 'If it's any consolation I don't think I'll sleep much myself, either.'

He moved towards her, then stopped dead, scowling, his hands clenched at his sides. 'Catherine, go inside now and close your door against me, *por favor*. A man can only endure so much!'

* * *

After a restless, frustrated night Catherine got up early next morning, full of high-minded resolution about her future conduct where Eduardo was concerned. From now on, she informed her reflection, you can just be sensible, my girl. No more kisses, no more tête-à-têtes. But even as she gave herself a list of dos and don'ts her hands were busy with her hair and face, making herself as attractive as possible to face Eduardo across the breakfast table. She pulled on a baggy yellow T-shirt over her white jersey trousers, slid her bare feet into comfortable brown leather loafers and went running down the spiral stairs, so eager to see Eduardo again that she forgot all about ghosts in the bright autumn sunshine.

But when she reached the *sala* Fernanda was the only one there, bustling about as she laid the small breakfast table. Catherine, deflated, lied about her night's sleep, refused offers of an English breakfast and somehow managed to keep back a query about Eduardo's whereabouts. When Fernanda hurried off Catherine went out on to the balcony to look down into the courtyard and over the fields beyond. Men were at work in the distance, but Eduardo was nowhere to be seen. Perhaps he had slept well after all, she thought, feeling very put out by the thought. She turned, her pulse quickening at the sound of footsteps, but the new arrival was Ana, radiant and glowing in jeans and jersey with a bright scarf tied at the neck.

'*Bom dia*,' she cried, kissing Catherine on both cheeks. 'How are you today?'

Catherine assured her she was very well, smiling brightly to hide her disappointment when she saw that the table was laid for only two. Eduardo, it seemed, was not expected for breakfast.

She was right. While Ana consumed yoghurt, an apple and a warm sweet roll, along with several cups of coffee, she chattered like a magpie. First she demanded an opinion of her Carlos, and smiled happily when Catherine told her sincerely that he was one of the most charming men she'd ever met. It was some time before Ana thought to mention that Eduardo had risen early to drive to Viana do Castelo to the *loja* there.

'*Loja?*' queried Catherine.

'The antiques shop my brother Pedro bought from a friend shortly before—before the accident. It sells porcelain, pictures also, and does very well now, but it gave Eduardo many problems before he made it into a success. It is yet another call on his time.' Ana sighed. 'He works so hard.' She cast an assessing eye at Catherine. 'You like him?'

To her annoyance Catherine felt heat rush into her face, and busied herself with the teapot. 'Of course I do. He's your brother, isn't he?'

'He likes *you* very much, I think.'

'Good.'

'You are blushing.'

'Nonsense!' Catherine made a face at the other girl. 'Now, what can I do to help, Ana? As far as the wedding's concerned?'

Ana smiled eagerly. 'Will you play chauffeur today, *querida*? If you drive me to Pontalegre we can visit the market this morning, then we can lunch at Casa das Camelias. This afternoon the *costureira* is bringing my wedding dress for the final fitting!'

When Catherine had been directed to the Pontalegre town house by a less vertical route than Eduardo's, Ana had a word with Elsa, then hurried with Catherine down the steep narrow streets to plunge into the noise and hubbub of market day.

The fortnightly *feira* in Pontalegre was an amazing sight to behold, transforming the normally tranquil little town into a gigantic *caravanserai*, the sandy shores of the river hidden from view beneath a great mass of white awnings which shaded stalls from the sun. The noise and bustle filled the bright morning air as people thronged the noisy cattle sale in full swing to one side of the bridge, or crowded the walkways between the stalls on the other side to indulge in spirited bargaining with vendors extolling the virtues of everything under the sun from fine ceramics, embroidery, jewellery and leather goods, to simple pottery and homely pots and pans, fresh vegetables and squawking poultry.

Ana darted from one stall to another, pointing out bargains until Catherine's brain reeled as she tried to decide which particular embroidered place-mats would please her mother most. To give her time to ponder Ana whisked her off to drink coffee under an umbrella at one of the tables in the main square, where the ancient fountain was ringed with potted plants by a vendor availing himself of the sparkling water supply to keep his wares fresh all day long.

After drinking two cups of the delicious local coffee in quick succession Catherine felt revived enough to dive back into the fray, and it was more than two hours later before the girls toiled up through the steep cobbled streets to the house, laden with her spoils.

'I hope I haven't worn you out?' said Catherine later, as they lunched on the balcony outside the *sala*.

'I feel wonderful!' declared Ana, her glowing looks supporting her words as she peeled an orange for Catherine with skill only a little less deft than her brother's. 'It is you who look tired, *querida*. Perhaps you did not sleep as well as you said, *não é?*'

'No,' admitted Catherine with a grin. 'I shouldn't have taken that nap yesterday.'

'Did you stay up late with Eduardo?'

'Not very.'

Ana eyed her challengingly, head on one side. 'He is not usually *so* attentive to guests, you understand!'

'Stop it, you monkey!' To divert her Catherine began laying out her purchases on the table. She grinned as she unwrapped a pair of amber ceramic oxen complete with cart. 'I couldn't resist them, nor these filigree earrings.' She threaded them through her ears then pushed her hair behind her ears, holding out her face for inspection. 'How do I look?'

'Beautiful as always,' said Ana simply. 'How could Eduardo help falling in love with you?'

'Ana!' Catherine collected her spoils together, frowning. 'I'm only here for a holiday. I've no intention of falling in love with anyone.'

Ana crowed in triumph. 'But I said Eduardo was *apaixonado*, Catherine—not you!'

When the dressmaker arrived with Ana's dress excitement pervaded the entire house as the two young maids crowded into the *sala* with Elsa to join in the fun. Their young faces shone with delight as the smart, black-clad Dona Lidia carefully drew the gown over Ana's head, then fastened it and pulled it into place.

The black velvet dress itself was simple, with a high neck, long sleeves and a plain bodice cut to outline Ana's curves. But the skirt won a low whistle of admiration from Catherine. Long and full, the entire surface was encrusted with gold beads interspersed with horizontal rows of gold embroidered flowers, leaves and hearts.

'Ana!' she breathed in awe. 'It's incredible! You look wonderful.'

A beaming Ana twirled slowly while the maids clapped and Catherine communicated in sign language with the dressmaker to convey her opinion of the exquisite workmanship.

By the time coffee and cakes had been consumed, the dressmaker congratulated and thanked profusely as she departed, and the dress hung lovingly away in Ana's room, it was late afternoon.

Ana caught her hand, suddenly serious for once. 'Ah, Catherine, I am so glad to have you here to share such things with me like this.'

Catherine hugged her wordlessly, both girls close to tears for a moment before Ana's smile lit her face again.

'Come. Let me show you the rooms we let to visitors before the new ones arrive.'

Two bedrooms were kept for paying guests, each of them with a pair of carved wooden beds, a bathroom, and doors leading out on the balcony which ran along the façade of the house. Each room had a small round table and chairs, vases of flowers, pieces of antique furniture, and, to Catherine's delight, a small iron stove, complete with a flue which went up through the ceiling.

'This is for curiosity only,' said Ana, indicating discreet radiators. 'Eduardo has installed heating in these rooms, but thought it of interest to keep the stoves.'

'He's right!'

'Eduardo is always right,' agreed Ana, resigned, then gave Catherine a saucy grin. 'Which is why I long for him to be *pernas para o ar.*'

'What on earth is that?'

'Head over heels! It would do him good.'

'I thought you said he had a thing going with this solicitor friend of his,' Catherine said carefully.

Ana shrugged as they returned along the shadowy corridor to the family's living quarters. 'I am certain it is no great romance. Eduardo has never lost his heart. Unless he has done so *very* recently,' she added wickedly.

When they arrived back at Quinta das Lagoas Ana eyed Catherine closely as they parted in the *sala*. 'You must rest, *querida*. There are shadows under those great golden eyes of yours. The car is not back so Eduardo has not returned yet. I shall knock on your door later to make sure you do not sleep too long.'

After the heat and dust of the market Catherine was only too pleased to have time to make herself more presentable before she met Eduardo again. But as she lingered in a cool bath she frowned. After teasing Ana about taking so much time to make herself beautiful for Carlos, she was now doing exactly the same thing herself, with nothing like the same justification. Eduardo was *not* her *noivo*, nor even her lover, nor ever likely to be.

The time before dinner passed with agonising slowness, yet in the end so much of it was spent in deliberation over what to wear that when Ana popped her head round the door a little after seven-thirty Catherine was still in her white silk teddy, wielding a hairbrush energetically in front of the mirror.

'*Nossa Senhora*, it is a good thing I did not allow Eduardo to come for you as he wished!' laughed Ana.

Catherine bent swiftly, brushing her mane of hair from nape to crown to hide the red tide of colour in her face. 'He's home?' she asked in a muffled voice.

'Yes. He is waiting for us in the *sala*. Dinner is earlier tonight. I shall sit here on the bed while you dress, *querida*.'

Catherine was glad of Ana's company, in no mood to go down alone tonight. After the heat and emotion of their parting the night before she could feel the same paralysing shyness threatening at the thought of facing Eduardo again. Doing her best to hide the shiver which ran through her at the memory of his kisses, she left her hair loose in response to Ana's plea, and was soon ready in a slim black dress with a brilliant gold silk handkerchief trailing from a hip pocket.

'You have learned to dress so well,' said Ana in admiration.

'I've got the cruise job to thank for that,' said Catherine as they went downstairs. 'It was part of the deal to look smart in the shop.'

When they reached the *sala* Eduardo was outside on the veranda, watching the moon rise. He turned at the sound of footsteps, moving to join them without haste, yet something in the way he looked at Catherine told her without words that his pulse was racing in unison with her own.

'*Boa tarde*, Catherine,' he said very quietly, raising her hand to his lips. 'You are, as always, a delight to the eye. I trust you do not object to my informality? Tonight I wished to relax.'

Catherine smiled, privately of the opinion that Eduardo looked even better tonight in pale linen trousers and shirt than in his formal suit of the night before. 'Of course not. Good evening. Have you had a very tiring day?'

'Very tiring!' said Ana, rushing to help Fernanda as the latter came in with a laden tray. 'Eduardo has interviewed several replacements for me.'

Fernanda sniffed. '*Todas casadas*!'

Eduardo eyed her challengingly. 'Are you against employment of married women, then, Fernanda?'

'*Pois sou*. They would be thinking of husbands and children instead of helping you with the *turistas*,' stated Fernanda, with the privileged licence of one long allowed opinions on family matters.

'*You* are married,' pointed out Ana wickedly.

'That is different,' said Fernanda indignantly. 'I live here, *meu marido* Manoel also. If she is married a *secretaria* will always be wanting to leave early, or arrive late——'

'If you have quite finished telling me how I should conduct my affairs, Fernanda,' interrupted Eduardo crisply, 'could you now serve dinner, *por favor*?'

'*Sim, Senhor*! *Agora mesma*,' said Fernanda with dignity, and departed, head held high.

'You have offended her, Eduardo,' said Ana, pulling a face.

Eduardo pulled out Catherine's chair, unmoved. 'It does no harm to make it clear to Fernanda occasionally just who is master here.'

'No one is ever in doubt about that,' Ana assured him. 'But Fernanda means no harm—she has been part of our lives since I was born, remember.'

'I do. But *she* must remember that it is I who make the decisions.' Eduardo turned to Catherine. 'Forgive us, *por favor*. Won't you try some of these *bolinhos de bacalhau*? It is said there are as many ways of preparing our famous salt cod as the days of the year.'

'This way is the best!' said Ana. 'Fernando makes the best *bolinhos* in the Minho.'

The hot morsels of deep-fried cod and potato were delicious, but so filling that Catherine was glad she'd resisted the temptation to eat more than one or two when confronted with the *cosido a Portuguesa* which followed.

'I don't know how anyone in this country ever stays even moderately slim,' said Catherine ruefully, eyeing the rich mixture of vegetables cooked with various meats and sausage.

'You have little cause for concern on such a subject,' commented Eduardo.

'Ah, but I haven't been here long!'

'Which reminds me. Since you are too busy with wedding preparations to play tourist with Catherine, do you not agree, Ana,' said Eduardo casually, 'that your friend should remain for a while after the wedding to explore our region of Portugal?'

Ana looked at him, arrested. '*Pois é*—of course, if Catherine wishes.'

'I shall remove to Casa das Camelias and leave Catherine in Fernanda's care at night,' went on Eduardo, as if it was a foregone conclusion, 'then by day I shall help her discover all the delights of our beautiful Minho.'

Sorely tempted by the idea, Catherine nevertheless took exception to Eduardo's supreme confidence in her consent. 'I'm afraid that's just not possible,' she said firmly. 'I must get back to my job-hunting in England. Besides...' She paused.

Both pairs of dark eyes turned on her in enquiry.

'Besides what, *querida*?' asked Ana.

'It is plain that Catherine has no wish to stay,' said Eduardo, pushing away his plate.

'It isn't that at all.' Catherine felt her colour rising, annoyed with him for bringing up such an emotive subject in front of Ana, who was plainly agog at the sudden tension in the atmosphere. 'But my flight is booked for Saturday week. I really *can't* stay.'

Eduardo's eyes frosted over as they stared into hers. 'Then of course there is no more to be said.'

'But thank you very much for the invitation,' she added belatedly, chilled to the bone by his sudden hauteur.

'*De nada.*' Eduardo pressed her to cheese and fruit with his usual faultless manners, but contributed very little more to the conversation for the rest of the meal. When they reached the coffee stage he glanced at his watch and rose to his feet. '*Com licenca.* I shall take my coffee to the study. Tonight I must go over the accounts I brought from Viana do Castelo. If I am to seek my bed before dawn I must begin at once.'

And to Catherine's dismay Eduardo gave an unsmiling, perfunctory bow and strode from the room.

Ana tut-tutted in surprise. '*Que coisa*! Eduardo is in *such* a bad mood—please forgive him, Catherine.'

Catherine assured her there was nothing to forgive, but secretly she was furious with Eduardo for ruining the evening. The Condo de Pontalegre, it was plain, was accustomed to people who fell in with his wishes the moment they were uttered.

Without Eduardo Catherine found the evening lacked much of its savour, and was guilty at her secret relief when Fernanda arrived later with a tea-tray.

'For Dona Caterina,' she announced, putting it down in front of Catherine. 'Senhor Eduardo ordered it for her.'

'How kind!' Catherine smiled gratefully. 'But I hope it hasn't kept you up, Fernanda? If I want tea I can easily make it myself.'

'*De maneira nenhuma, señhora,*' said the woman loftily. '*O Senhor Conde mandou*. He gives the orders. I obey.'

Ana sighed as Fernanda bade them goodnight and marched off to her quarters. 'She is still cross with Eduardo. She only refers to him as "Senhor Conde" when she is mad at him.'

Since Catherine wasn't exactly pleased with Eduardo either she made no comment as she offered Ana some tea.

'*Não, obrigada.*' Ana yawned sleepily.

'Why don't you pop off to bed? I'll just drink this, then I'll go up to my room to read.' Catherine grinned. 'Carlos won't want a bride with nasty dark marks under her eyes, remember!'

'*E verdade.*' Ana kissed Catherine on both cheeks, argued a little about staying up, but at last went off to her room downstairs, plainly glad to get to bed.

Catherine slowly drank one cup of tea, then another she didn't want, hoping against hope that Eduardo would appear before she'd finished. When it became mortifyingly obvious that he was going to do no such thing she took the tray downstairs to the kitchen and washed up. Afterwards the *sala* remained obstinately deserted, and with a sigh Catherine went through to the hall, which was in its usual semi-darkness, with moonlight filtering through the windows.

She hesitated, eyeing the study door in the far corner. When it remained shut she walked briskly across the stone flags to the stairs, hoping the click of her heels might bring Eduardo from his lair, but nothing happened. Catherine made a face at the closed door and switched on the stair lights, but after a quick flash they went off, as though a fuse had blown somewhere. She frowned. This, surely, was a good enough excuse to seek out Eduardo. On the other hand in his present mood he'd probably just provide her with a candle and send her on her way, with one of those daunting bows of his. Depressed, she began making her way up the stairs in the dark, suddenly uneasy as she remembered Eduardo's mention of ghosts.

Steeling herself, Catherine went carefully up the dark spiral, longing to race up the winding steps, but forced to feel for each one with the toe of her shoe as she went. On the first landing a small window let in a little moonlight to make things easier, but as she climbed upwards again into Stygian darkness Catherine's heart gave a sickening thump. She stopped dead, certain she could hear something. Gritting her teeth, she forced herself up the last few steps towards a glimmer of moonlight, then gave a screech of horror as she collided with a figure barring her way at the top. She lashed out wildly, panic rendering her deaf to Eduardo's voice as he caught her in his arms.

'*Deus*, Catherine it is I! Do not fight so. I did not mean to frighten you.'

'Then why the devil were you lurking here in the dark?' she panted furiously, struggling to free herself.

'Because I wished to speak with you before you went to bed.' He tightened his hold. 'No. I will not release you. Be still.'

Catherine glared at him, incensed. 'If you wanted to see me, why didn't you come to the *sala*?'

'Because Ana was there. I wished to talk to you alone.'

'Are you sure you mean *talk*?' she said scathingly, and at once she was free.

Eduardo stepped back, the disdain on his face blazingly obvious despite the dim light. 'I have never found it necessary to force my attentions on a woman. I shall not begin with you, Catherine.'

Catherine stood in silence for an interval, arms hugged across her chest as her thumping heart quietened. 'No, I know,' she admitted at last. 'I'm sorry. But you scared the living daylights out of me. It's all your fault, with your talk of ghosts last night. For a moment I thought you were some dead Barroso ancestor come to haunt me.'

He smiled faintly. 'Instead you find a live Barroso. Very much alive, I warn, since in spite of my assurances there is nothing I desire more than to take you in my arms, Catherine. But I shall not. Unless,' he added softly, 'you give me a sign that it is your wish.'

Catherine's chin lifted. 'Why should I do that?'

'Why, indeed?' He leaned his shoulders against the stone wall. 'Therefore let us talk. Or let *me* talk, Catherine. I wish to apologise for my behaviour earlier.'

'For marching off like a sulky schoolboy when I refused to fall in with your plan, you mean!'

'*Exatamente.*' He inclined his head. 'It seemed to me so reasonable and delightful a plan, you understand. It was like cold water thrown in my face to have you refuse. Also I was frustrated, unable to persuade you as I wished because of Ana's presence. *Então*, I shut myself away in my study.'

Catherine eyed him challengingly. 'Did you get your work done?'

He smiled. 'Yes. *De verdade*, it did not take long.' He came away from the wall to stand erect. 'But after insisting I had so much to do my pride would not allow me to return to the *sala*.'

'Is your pride so important to you, then?'

'*Sem duvida*. Without pride a man is not a man!' Eduardo moved a little, barring the way to the tower bedroom. 'Is there truly no way I can persuade you to remain after the wedding, Catherine? It would so greatly please me to show you some of my beloved Minho. It is said, you understand, to be the cradle of Portugal—not merely the place where I was born, but the birthplace of my entire country.'

With the stairs cutting off her retreat Catherine had no option but to stand her ground. 'I would like to stay very much,' she sighed at last. 'But it just isn't possible, Eduardo. I need to go home to find a job, my flight is booked, my mother is expecting me, there's a whole list of reasons why I really must go.' And top of the list is because if I stay, she added silently, you'll put such a dent in my heart, it would take more than a bit of globe-trotting to mend it this time.

'None of these reasons would be important if you really wished to stay,' said Eduardo very quietly. 'Tell me the truth, Catherine. This—this bond I feel between us. Do you really not feel it too?'

Her eyes fell. 'You know I do. Otherwise——'

He seized her by the elbows. 'Otherwise you would not have surrendered so sweetly to my kisses! Is that not true?'

She nodded dumbly, and he drew her slowly towards him until she rested against his chest, the thud of his heartbeat loud against her cheek. Eduardo's arms locked about her, his breath exuded in a long, relishing sigh as he laid his cheek against her hair.

The silence on the small, moonlit landing was absolute. Nothing stirred in the quiet night. Their isolation enclosed them in such alluring intimacy that Catherine, at first lulled into security by the sheer comfort of the embrace, gradually came alive to danger. Her pulse began to race as she sensed the sudden tension in Eduardo's hard, muscular body, felt the stirring, unmistakable evidence of his desire pressing against her. She shied away in alarm, but Eduardo recaptured her easily, one arm hard about her waist, his free hand moving down her spine to mould her even closer against him as his mouth sought hers.

At the touch of his lips Catherine knew herself defeated. Her bones seemed affected by some new plasticity, she the clay and he the sculptor as his hands moved over her, exploring every curve and hollow, bringing her to restless, responsive life. She could feel the now familiar urgency in him, like an electric current flowing from his body into hers, as Eduardo took infinite pleasure in arousing her to a sexual response she had never dreamed of, much less experienced. His confident, invading fingers slid buttons from their moorings, smoothed silk aside to reach the golden skin beneath as he eased her back gently against the wall, his mouth leaving hers to descend in a heart-stopping trail to find breasts which hardened, thrusting in response as he cupped them in suddenly unsteady hands. She stiffened, her neck arching as his lips closed on taut, expectant nipples so sensitive to his tongue and teeth that Catherine gave a choked, protesting cry. She trembled violently as Eduardo's hair brushed against her heated skin, his mouth continuing its relentless attention to each swollen bud in turn, sending arrows of fiery response to the molten target of desire burning deep inside her.

At the precise moment the exquisite torture became too much to bear he caught her up against him, his mouth crushing hers. For a few stormy moments they stood together, mouth to mouth and breast to breast, their arms about each other in convulsive, rib-threatening grip. At last Catherine tore her mouth away and Eduardo raised his head, his eyes glittering into hers in the moonlight, his ragged breathing hot against her cheek.

'Now you know why I won't stay,' she panted at last. 'If I do——' She made a helpless little gesture.

'If you do you know we shall become lovers,' he said harshly, emotion emphasising his accent. 'You do not desire this?'

Catherine wanted it more than she'd ever wanted anything in her entire life, but it seemed hardly the moment to say so. She knew, beyond all doubt, that given the slightest encouragement Eduardo would forget she was a guest beneath his roof, forget his vows about her safety, and behave exactly as any other red-blooded male would in the same circumstances.

Yet even held close in his arms, his heart thundering against hers, Catherine recognised, with terrifying clarity, that what she felt for Eduardo was a great deal more than any mere mindless response of the body. Her mind and heart were already so much in tune with her senses where Eduardo Barroso was concerned that it was useless to tell herself that this man was virtually a stranger. She shivered, burying her head against his shoulder. For the first time in her life she knew exactly what was meant by the true meaning of the word 'lover', embodied with exactitude in the charismatic person of the man waiting impatiently for her answer.

Catherine raised her head to look up into his taut, expectant face. 'Whatever my feelings,' she said unsteadily, 'we can't let it happen. We hardly know each other——'

'Then why will you not stay, Catherine, so we may learn to know each other better?'

'No, Eduardo.' She swallowed hard. 'Oh, lord, this is so hard to explain! Can't you understand that if we become lovers, Eduardo, it would ruin my life?'

He stared at her, outraged, his fingers biting into her shoulders. '*Por que*? Why do you say this? I would never hurt you, *meu amor*——'

'You wouldn't *mean* to,' she cried desperately. 'But you would, just the same.' She saw his face harden at her words, felt him withdraw slightly, and she clutched at his shirt front. 'Eduardo, please! Don't go all aloof and aristocratic on me.'

Eduardo glared down at her for an instant longer then relaxed, his eyes softening. 'Ah, *querida*, do not look so. I will do whatever you wish. If we are to have only this short time together, there must be no shadow cast on it for you, nor for Ana.'

'Then we can go back to being friends?'

'Catherine, I cannot think of you as just a friend!' He touched her cheek. 'Why—*why* do you say I would ruin your life?'

She sighed heavily. 'In words of one syllable, Eduardo Barroso, a short holiday spent in your company would be just a nice little interlude for you. For me it would be something else entirely.'

'Explain,' he ordered.

'Because it would probably spoil me for any other man in future, of course. There! I hope you're satisfied.'

'That is truly how you feel?' he asked very quietly.

Regretting her candour already, Catherine nodded and opened her door. 'It is. So I'll go back where I belong before—before it's too late. Goodnight, Eduardo.' She frowned as he pressed a switch beside the door, flooding the landing with light. 'Odd! When I switched them on downstairs they fused.'

He smiled triumphantly. 'It is a two-way switch, *queridinha*. You turned it on—I turned it off again.'

Catherine's eyes flashed. 'Just so you could lie in ambush to frighten the life out of me?'

Eduardo laughed, unrepentant. 'I confess I hoped you would seek protection in my arms from ghosts who lurk in the shadows.'

'It worked very well, didn't it? What a fool I am.'

'Ah, no, Catherine.' He raised her hand to his lips. 'If this were true I would not experience so strong a feeling of rapport. For me a woman's beauty is by no means her most important attribute. Perhaps I ask too much, but a woman must also have a mind—a heart—a soul—if God is good, even a sense of humour.' In between each word he kissed a separate finger, then stood looking down at her, still holding her hand. 'Now I must leave you, *não é*?'

'Yes. You must. Goodnight.' Catherine detached her hand gently, bracing herself to say that which had to be said. 'Eduardo.'

'Yes, Catherine?'

She breathed in deeply, her eyes holding his. 'Will you turn to ice again if I say that from now on we'd better avoid being alone together?'

His face darkened. 'How could I turn to ice? Whenever I am near you I burn, Catherine——'

'Which only proves my point,' she said wildly. 'All this is too—too sudden. If we go on like this it's bound to end in tears. For me, anyway.'

He made a swift move towards her then stood still, his arms falling at his sides. 'I do not agree!' he said tersely. 'Yet I will do whatever you wish. I have no desire to cause you tears, Catherine.'

'Thank you.' She smiled sadly. 'You won't stay away from me altogether, I hope?'

'How could I? For the cruelly short time you are here,' he added, in a tone which took her breath away, 'I desire to spend every waking hour with you, *querida*, and if this means I must keep Ana with us all the time then so be it. I would sell my soul to spend every sleeping hour with you also,' he added hoarsely, his eyes burning like coals in his set face. '*Boa noite*, Catherine. Sleep well.' He thrust her through her bedroom door, then raced down the ancient stone stairs at breakneck speed, as though to outrun his overpowering desire to stay.

CHAPTER SIX

CATHERINE went downstairs next morning in some trepidation, uncertain what to expect from Eduardo after the manner of their parting. But to her relief the man who joined his sister and her guest for breakfast was a different man from the offended autocrat who'd left the dinner table the night before. Ignoring Ana's mock-pious thanks for the miracle, he kissed her cheek, smiled at Catherine with a warmth so deliberate that all her fears evaporated, then set himself to the task of wooing Fernanda from her offended dignity. After watching Fernanda capitulate with barely a struggle, quickly her normal bossy self again as she served the meal, Catherine applied herself to her breakfast very pensively. If his sister and housekeeper had no defence against Eduardo's charm, there was precious little chance for someone like herself, shaking inside like a jelly right this minute just because his shoe was in deliberate contact with hers under the breakfast table.

Catherine soon learned that Eduardo meant to comply meticulously with her request of the night before. Immediately after breakfast he announced he had business in Cascais with the travel agents who put many of the Barroso paying guests their way, and suggested Ana take Catherine to Viana do Castelo for a day's shopping and sightseeing.

'Tomorrow,' he promised, 'I shall take time off to accompany you both wherever you wish.'

96

Catherine's feelings during the next few days see-sawed between relief and regret as Eduardo obeyed her wishes to the letter. As a host he was charming and unfailing in his attentions, but spent no more time alone in Catherine's company. And, though this was exactly what she'd begged for, secretly she was disappointed. Deep down she had never really expected Eduardo to fall in with her suggestion quite so whole-heartedly. He was in her company most of the time, it was true, and appointed himself guide on several expeditions, but apart from an occasional touch of the hand, or eyes which suddenly locked for a heart-thumping instant, Catherine began to wonder if she'd imagined the dangerous delight of the lovemaking which had forced her to plead for the present truce. A truce which Eduardo, to her mortification, seemed to be keeping to with no apparent effort.

The days passed in a hectic programme of excursions and sightseeing, Catherine's camera working overtime as she visited the Thursday market in Barcelos to buy delicate pieces of pottery, the dunes of Ofir to swim, the wooded hill outside Braga to see the gigantic fan-like staircase of the shrine of Bom Jesus, where they paused on every landing so that Catherine could photograph the fountains and statues and chapels on the climb to the baroque church at the top. But underlying her pleasure in it all Catherine suffered secret pangs of guilt because her degree of enjoyment on the various expeditions was in exact ratio to whether Eduardo came along or not.

Some evenings Carlos joined them for dinner, on others Eduardo took them out for a meal in Pontalegre or to Arcos de Valdevez, where at the Adega Nacional Catherine discovered the delights of an *Espetada de*

Lulas—the house speciality of squid cooked with bacon on a spit. Sunday was spent with the da Cunha family at the Quinta da Floresta so that Catherine could see Ana's future home. Carlos's family were a lively crowd, his brothers and sisters younger than himself, and his parents kind, charming people who welcomed Ana's English friend with effortless hospitality. It was late when Eduardo drove them back to the Quinta, where to Catherine's surprise he suggested that a sleepy Ana go straight to bed.

'You look tired, *carinha*. I shall stay with Catherine while she drinks her bedtime cup of tea.'

'Oh, but you needn't——' began Catherine, but Ana quelled her protests with a sleepy hug.

'Eduardo is delighted to keep you company,' she said firmly, and wandered off to bed, yawning.

The silence she left behind her in the *sala* was tense. Eduardo looked at the tray Fernanda had left ready for Catherine and smiled slightly. 'Will you trust me to make your tea, Catherine?'

'No!' Catherine bit her lip, unable to meet his eyes. 'I mean I don't really want any tea tonight. I—I think I'll follow Ana's example and go straight to bed.'

Eduardo barred her way, his face sardonic. 'What exactly do you fear? I will not eat you, Catherine. *Deus me livre*, I have been so tame, so docile of late. I have done exactly as you wish. Although there were moments this past week when I felt I would go mad if I did not have you to myself. Do you think it was *easy*?'

'It certainly seemed to be,' said Catherine tartly, then could have kicked herself as she saw the gleam in his eyes.

'This annoyed you?' he said softly.

'Of course not!'

'I was merely complying with your wishes,' he reminded her. 'If my kisses frighten you I apologise, Catherine. But you lie if you say the desire was mine alone.'

'It wasn't,' she said flatly. 'That, Eduardo Barroso, was the trouble. I'd never felt like that before—ever— and it scared me to death. I was afraid . . .' She halted, unable to face the leap of desire in his eyes.

'You were afraid we would become lovers,' he finished for her.

She nodded dumbly.

'This would be such a bad thing?'

'Yes. Because I'm convinced you want me for the wrong reasons!'

They faced each other like adversaries.

'What reason could there be,' he demanded hotly, 'except for the rapport we feel, for the bond I feel tying me to you——?'

'But that's just what I *am* saying!' she cried. 'This bond isn't just to do with me, Catherine Ward. I'd never be sure that it was me you really wanted, or whether you were trying to re-live some adolescent dream you once had of Isabel Cardoso!'

She flung the words at him as if they were a gauntlet. Eduardo moved to seize her, then stood still, his hands clenched in white-knuckled fists at his side.

'You are wrong!' He breathed in deeply. 'Catherine, if you will not drink tea, will you perhaps join me in a whisky, or some wine? For once I have very real need of a drink, and tonight I do not wish to drink alone.'

Catherine looked at him thoughtfully, then nodded. 'A very small glass of port, then.'

'Thank you.' He waved her to the sofa. 'I think it is time we exorcise the ghost of Isabel. Since by some whim of fate you have her face it is only right, *de certeza*, that you should know her story.'

Not sure that she really wanted to, Catherine eyed him uneasily. 'Are you certain you want to tell me? I mean, if it's some private family matter——'

'It is private, yes,' he agreed, and let himself down with a sigh beside her. 'But I wish you to hear it.'

Catherine made no protest when he took her hand in his, glad of the warm contact as he began to talk, very quietly at first, pausing to frown in concentration as he cast his mind back to the events which had taken place so many years before.

When Isabel Cardoso arrived to make her home with the Barrosos the family consisted of the Conde and Condessa, their eldest son Pedro, away at Coimbra University, twelve-year-old Eduardo and his sisters Maria Leonor and Maria Cristina, several years his junior. Ana Maria had some time to wait before her appearance on the scene.

Isabel, a cousin of the Condessa's, was just eighteen years old, motherless from birth, and recently orphaned by the death of her elderly father. She came to the Quinta das Lagoas straight from the convent where she'd just completed her education.

'To me she was all the princesses in all the fairytales I had ever read. I fell madly in love with her, young though I was,' said Eduardo ruefully.

In return for her inclusion in the Barroso household the grateful Isabel, who had been an industrious student, took on the role of governess to the Barroso children.

'I was enchanted by her,' said Eduardo without drama. 'One look from those crystal eyes of hers and I would do anything she asked.'

Not, he emphasised, that Isabel asked anything of the children other than their attention to their lessons. Eduardo, older than his sisters, and a schoolboy, was naturally not included in these, but eagerly joined in all the leisure activities presided over by his beautiful cousin whenever he could.

'The short time she lived with us,' said Eduardo, 'was an idyllic period in my life.'

'She wasn't with you very long, then?' said Catherine. 'I suppose she met someone fairly quickly?'

Eduardo's expressive mouth twisted. 'This was the tragedy. Isabel fell madly in love, *de certeza*. Unfortunately the object of her passion did not return it.'

When Pedro came home on vacation from Coimbra he met Isabel for the first time since their childhood. He was carefree, charming and darkly handsome, and to Isabel, convent-bred with no experience of men, quite literally the answer to a maiden's prayer.

Eduardo's grasp tightened as he said that one night the moonlight had kept him awake in the bedroom now occupied by Catherine in the tower. The young Eduardo, curled up on the window-seat, watched as Pedro appeared in the courtyard below, lit one of the cigars forbidden by his mother, then strolled off through the arch into the *campo*, the tip of his cigar making it easy to follow his progress.

'He did this most nights,' said Eduardo. 'He would creep out in secret, believing no one knew.' He gave a soft, mirthless laugh. 'I can remember my secret glee, as I planned to plague him next day. Then to my astonishment I saw Isabel, following him like a ghost in the moonlight, a shawl flung over her nightgown. To this day I can recall my deep distress, the instinct which recognised that what Isabel was doing was wrong.'

To complete the young Eduardo's misery he saw his mother emerge from the house as Isabel went down on her knees in supplication to his brother, her hair flowing down her back like a dark veil.

'I could hear no words,' went on Eduardo. 'But young as I was I could tell, even from that distance, that Pedro was astonished by Isabel's behaviour. When he saw my mother he embraced her in relief, but Isabel buried her face in her hands, sobbing in despair. My mother raised her, comforting her, then held out her free hand to Pedro. I was in tears myself as I saw him kiss my mother's hand in homage before escorting her into the house with Isabel.'

Catherine waited, her eyes on Eduardo's brooding, introspective face.

'Was Isabel sent away?' she asked tentatively at last.

He shook his head. 'No. Pedro told me, years later, that my mother was a saint to Isabel that night. She put the frantic girl to bed, administered restoratives and comforted her, remained with her until she seemed calm. Only then did my mother confront Pedro in his room to ask if Isabel's passion was truly one-sided. Pedro assured her he felt only a brother's affection for Isabel, that he would never dream of seducing a young girl under his parents' protection.' Eduardo raked a hand through his hair. 'When she was missing from her room next morning there was a search.

Eventually they found Isabel in one of the pools which give the Quinta its name.'

Catherine shuddered. 'Poor, poor girl! How tragic.' She looked up at him bleakly. 'If this face of mine is so like hers no wonder you were struck dumb at the sight of me. I'm sorry I brought back such painful memories.'

Eduardo's eyes softened. 'It is no fault of yours, Catherine. But I crave a boon of you. Only I know the truth of what happened. My little sisters were told Isabel had gone to heaven in the night. Ana was not even born then. She knows only that you bear this extraordinary resemblance to the young cousin who drowned herself for love. It is, *sem duvida*, the truth as far as it goes, so will you shield Ana from the fact that Pedro was involved?'

'Of course.' Catherine stared at their clasped hands. 'But will I meet any other people likely to think I'm a ghost?'

Eduardo shrugged. '*E possiviel*. But few people knew Isabel well. None of the servants of that time is still with us. Leonor and Cristina may remember enough to notice the resemblance, also one or two older relatives. But it will merely be a conversation piece. You and I are the only ones who know of Isabel's ill-fated passion for my brother, *gracas a Deus*.'

'Thank you for taking me into your confidence.'

He raised her hand to his lips. 'It is not my habit to relate family secrets to a stranger. But you have never, never been a stranger to me, Catherine, from the first moment I saw you.'

Her eyes widened. 'Eduardo, when did Isabel die exactly?'

'Twenty-three years ago this July——' He frowned at the look on her face. 'What is it?'

'It was my birthday in March,' she said, shivering. 'Exactly twenty-two years and nine months from the time she died.'

He pulled her into his arms, holding her close. 'I know what you are thinking—do not,' he said fiercely. 'You are yourself alone, Catherine Ward. The physical resemblance to Isabel is merely a coincidence. She was a foolish, romantic girl who did not expect to die. She was a devout Catholic, remember. Isabel would not have endangered her immortal soul by taking her own life. Most of the pools here are shallow. She knew this. Unfortunately there had been much rain and the one she chose was deeper than she realised. Pedro told me years later that she had even pinned a nosegay of *alecrim* to her dress.'

'*Alecrim*?'

'*Sim*. The herb used with the chicken we ate today. It is in Shakespeare's *Hamlet*.'

'Ah! Rosemary—for remembrance.'

'Isabel had studied Shakespeare at the convent. She liked *Hamlet* most of all.' Eduardo's mouth tightened. 'I believe she saw herself as Ophelia, and had some silly, girlish plan for Pedro to find her floating on the water, her hair streaming behind her, just like the illustration in her book of Shakespeare's plays.' His arms tightened. 'In a way her plan succeeded. It *was* Pedro who found her.'

Catherine shuddered. 'Oh, poor, poor boy! He didn't deserve that. It must have had an appalling effect on him.'

'*E verdade*. It changed his life. He was never the same again.'

They held each other close in silence, in an embrace totally devoid of passion as they sought solace from each other's nearness. It was a long time before Eduardo's arms finally fell away.

'Enough of past sorrows, Catherine,' he said at last. 'It is late and you must go to bed. My sisters and their families arrive in the morning, remember, and all peace at Quinta das Lagoas will be at an end.'

'I look forward to meeting them,' said Catherine, taking her cue from him. 'Perhaps I'd better pack my things tonight, ready for the move to Casa das Camelias tomorrow.'

Eduardo traced a finger down her cheek. 'There will be time enough in the morning. My sisters are not renowned for punctuality.'

'It's time I went to bed anyway,' said Catherine, putting her hand in his as he helped her to her feet. 'Goodnight, Eduardo.'

'Has Isabel's story made you sad?' he asked.

'A little. But I think I feel even sorrier for Pedro and your parents. They were left to deal with the aftermath of the tragedy, which must have been terrible for them.'

'*E verdade*. But do not think of it any more,' he said firmly. 'It all happened a long time ago. From now until Ana's wedding we must think only of happy things, *não é*?'

'Absolutely.' Catherine smiled a little. 'May I have my hand back now, please?'

There was no answering smile in his eyes. 'If you insist. Ah, Catherine, do you not think I have been virtuous these past days? Do I not deserve a reward for my obedience to your commands?'

Her smile grew mischievous. 'What would you like?'

Eduardo snatched her to him, his patience suddenly vanished. 'You have to ask?' he demanded thickly and kissed her with an intensity which set her heart hammering before he put her from him at last, his eyes glittering in his set face. 'Tonight I will not escort you to your bedroom door, Catherine.'

'You're abandoning me to your ghosts?' she asked unsteadily.

He gave a mirthless laugh. 'At this moment, *querida*, it shames me to confess you are safer with them than with me!'

Once breakfast was over next morning Catherine insisted on helping Ana and Fernanda prepare for the new arrivals.

'You are a guest. You need not do this,' said Eduardo, frowning in disapproval once Ana had gone to fetch bedlinen.

'I prefer to think of myself as Ana's friend than just a guest. Besides,' Catherine added tartly, 'if I want to help, Eduardo, I most certainly will!'

His eyes flashed for an instant, then softened as he smiled down into her challenging face. 'You do not offer to help me,' he pointed out. 'Yet I must work unaided in my office.'

'My heart aches for you!'

'As does mine for you—and not only my heart,' he muttered darkly, and strode swiftly from the room.

Catherine watched him go, aware that the amnesty was over, and guiltily pleased because of it. As she went with Ana later up the spiral stairs she consoled herself that it was no use worrying about life after

Eduardo. The only course open to her was to make the most of what she had right now, living each moment to the full until it was time for her to go.

It was fun to help Ana, who was surprisingly efficient, despite her light-hearted chatter, and soon the tower bedrooms and bathrooms were all in readiness, while Fernanda, with the help of a niece pressed into service for the occasion, dealt with the rooms below. When all was ready Catherine and Ana tidied themselves hastily, stowed Catherine's newly packed bags in her car, then collapsed in chairs on the veranda to drink coffee with Eduardo, who announced that he was giving himself a little holiday until the wedding was over.

Only half an hour later than expected—a record, according to Ana—the new arrivals turned in through the arch almost simultaneously, and sisters, brothers-in-law, children and maids disgorged themselves in utter pandemonium in the courtyard, with such a welter of kissing and embracing that Catherine doubted she would ever work out who belonged to whom as she was introduced.

Eventually the group resolved itself into two halves: Antonio Melo Viana, his wife Leonor, their daughters of seven and five and their baby son. The others were Mario Nogueira and his wife Cristina, with a family of two daughters and two sons, all under ten. Both women were elegant, friendly creatures who bore a marked family resemblance to Eduardo and Ana, and were only too happy to practise their rusty English on Catherine. The bride, however, after a quick inspection of her excited nieces' bridesmaids dresses, flatly refused to stay to lunch.

'Catherine and I must go,' she said firmly. 'Eduardo may stay if he wishes.'

'You are so kind,' murmured Eduardo drily. 'However, Elsa expects me at Casa das Camelias also—*não*, Raul,' he added to a small, clamouring nephew. He gave both small boys a quick hug. '*Futebol agora não!*' He kissed his pretty nieces then hurried Catherine and Ana down to the cars in the courtyard, grinning as they all waved to the assembled throng on the veranda. '*Meu Deus*, let us escape quickly—I am in no mood for a game of football!'

From that moment on wedding fever infected them all. At the town house Catherine settled quickly into the pretty back bedroom she was to share with Ana, ate a swift lunch, then lent a hand with some ironing as Ana packed, ready for her honeymoon in Paris. Later, when Eduardo was needed at the house to oversee the installation of extra lighting in the garden, Catherine volunteered to drive Ana to Oporto to transport wedding guests from the airport to the pretty modern hotel in the town.

'What happens if it rains?' asked Catherine, on the way to Oporto.

'God will not let it rain,' said Ana with calm certainty. 'I have prayed for sunshine.'

By the time the new arrivals had been collected and installed at the Albergaria overlooking the riverbank Catherine felt quite weary from the effects of a long drive coupled with enforced practice of her phrasebook Portuguese.

'My vocabulary isn't up to prolonged conversations,' she admitted ruefully, as they drove back to the house.

'I didn't realise you knew so much!' said Ana in admiration. 'You must rest before dinner—but first let us see what is happening in the garden.'

They found Eduardo stripped to the waist at the top of a ladder, personally arranging garlands of lights among the branches of the camellias.

'An ancestor of ours brought the trees from China,' he explained, climbing down to join them. 'Since I do not wish harm to come to them I decided to hang the lights myself.'

'*Eu posso ligar*?' begged Ana, and he laughed, patting her cheek. '*Sim, por favor*, switch them on, then.'

Expecting a vivid array of colours among the leaves, Catherine gazed in delight as the lights suddenly glowed against the deepening dusk, uniformly gold, as though the camellias had sprouted exotic, glowing fruit.

'Perfect!' she breathed, as Ana clapped her hands.

'*Perfeita, mesmo*,' agreed Eduardo in Catherine's ear, his bare chest brushing her shoulder, and she flushed, knowing without turning her head that his eyes were on her face instead of the lights.

Later that evening there was a lively family dinner with Eduardo's sisters and their husbands, the children left at the Quinta in the care of Fernanda and their nursemaids. The evening passed very pleasantly, with some family talk inevitable, but everyone careful to make the conversation as general as possible to include Catherine. The only awkward moment arose when Ana was summoned to the telephone for her regular nightly talk with Carlos.

Leonor, the older of the two sisters, looked thoughtful as she poured coffee in the comfortable little *sala* while the men smoked cigars outside on the veranda.

'Cristina, all night it puzzles me. I have such a strange feeling that I have met Catherine before.'

Her sister nodded, frowning. 'I have thought this also, at dinner. Yet Catherine says this is her first visit here.' She looked up as her brother re-entered the room. 'Eduardo, do you feel this also? Catherine, remember, *desculpe-me*,' she said to Catherine, 'my English is not used much these days.'

'You're saying I remind you of someone?' asked Catherine, taking the bull by the horns. 'Eduardo said the same when I first arrived. Apparently I resemble a cousin of yours, who died young.'

Neither woman looked convinced.

'Isabel Cardoso?' said Cristina doubtfully. '*E possiviel*—but we were small then, of course. I do not remember the poor girl clearly. *Coitadinha*—such a tragedy!'

'The likeness is very slight,' stated Eduardo firmly. 'Isabel's eyes were grey. Catherine's are the colour of the amber drops in her ears.'

His sisters, it was plain, had no recollection of Isabel's eyes, nor had they noticed Catherine's until now. They scrutinised their brother with sudden interest, but at that point Ana rejoined them, and the conversation turned to the arrivals of next day.

'It is a long time since I have seen Tia Clara,' observed Leonor, refilling Catherine's cup. 'I am glad I stay at the Quinta—she terrifies me. So does Antonia Soares, I confess—such a brain, that woman!'

Catherine sat very still, avoiding Eduardo's eye.

'Ah—I forgot,' he said casually, 'Antonia rang this afternoon, Ana, to say she regrets that a crisis with one of her cases prevents her from attending your wedding after all. She sends *abraços*, and wishes you every happiness. While we dined I instructed one of the maids to move Catherine's belongings to the room prepared for Antonia,' he added.

'You could have asked if Catherine wished to move!' said Ana indignantly.

Eduardo turned to Catherine with one of his graceful bows. '*Perdoneme*. My sole desire was to protect you from nights disturbed by attacks of bridal nerves from Ana.'

Catherine joined in the general outbreak of laughter at the mere thought of nerves of any kind from a bride so happy and enthusiastic about her forthcoming marriage. As the conversation became general Catherine found she felt tired. The slight strain of meeting so many new people, coupled with a secret, mortifying jealousy of the unknown Antonia, whether present or not, filled her with an urgent desire for her bed, wherever it was.

Ana, quick to note the shadow on Catherine's face, took her by the hand. 'Come, *querida*, you look tired. I am sure everyone will excuse us if we leave now. My sisters will talk for hours yet.'

At once the men were on their feet, their wives embracing Catherine warmly as they repeated their pleasure in making her acquaintance.

'I will escort the ladies to their rooms,' stated Eduardo, coolly ignoring the speculation in his sisters' eyes as he held the door for Catherine and Ana to pass through into the shadowy corridor outside. Once away from the others, Ana, correctly interpreting an imperious look from her brother, announced that she wanted a word with Elsa before going to bed. She kissed Catherine swiftly, wished her goodnight, then vanished into the servants' quarters.

Eduardo took Catherine by the elbow, hurrying her along the polished granite floor of the corridor and through the double doors that led into the sleeping quarters of the house. Outside the door of her new room he came to a halt, his eyes locking with hers.

'What is troubling you?' he demanded.

'Nothing.'

'*Bobagem*. Something is wrong. You have not looked at me since Antonia Soares was mentioned.'

Catherine's head came up haughtily. 'You're imagining it. Your friends are nothing to do with me.'

'*Escuta*—listen, Catherine. Antonia is an old friend. We were colleagues in Lisboa——'

Catherine tried to free herself. 'As I said, Eduardo, it's nothing to *do* with me.'

Eduardo released her elbows to pull her into his arms, but she resisted, standing like a ramrod in his grasp. 'You are wrong! It is everything to do with you. *Meu Deus*, can you not see that since our first meeting you fill my entire mind? I can think of no one but you!'

Heat rushed to her cheeks. 'And how would Miss Soares react to that?' she demanded, quailing slightly as his aquiline features hardened to an arrogance new to her.

'Since I do not intend to discuss so private and delicate a subject with her it is unlikely I shall know,' he said icily.

They eyed each other in silence, black gaze implacable as it held the defiant amber one, and at last Catherine gave a despairing sigh as she yielded to the arms urging her closer.

'This is crazy,' she muttered against his chest.

'I know it! I have tried to keep my distance from you, but it is no use. If to burn for you like this after so short a time is crazy, then I am mad.' He turned her face up to his. 'Yet will you believe that this is not just your body I want so desperately, *carinha*?'

Her eyes lit up, then dulled. 'I do believe it—but it makes no difference, Eduardo. You have to accept the fact that we'll never be lovers.'

He smiled, the heat in his dark eyes causing irreparable damage to her resistance. 'Never is a long time, Catherine,' he muttered before stopping her protests with a kiss meant to underline his statement.

She pushed at his arms feebly. 'You must go. Ana will be along in a minute. And the others will wonder what you're doing.'

'If they do they will not dare to say so!'

'Tyrant!'

He smiled. 'Never with you, *querida*.' He touched his lips to her cheek. 'From the moment I first looked into those golden eyes of yours I was your slave.'

In some small part of her mind Catherine knew that she should laugh, treat his extravagance as a joke, but it was beyond her. After the frustration of the past few days this unexpected privacy with Eduardo was heaven. Her fleeting jealousy vanished as she gave herself up to the pure joy of the stolen moment together. Her hands reached up to hold his head closer as their lips met once more, and she gasped as his urgent tongue invaded all the soft, secret recesses of her mouth in a penetration which inflamed them both to the point where Eduardo gave an agonised curse when Ana's voice from the stairwell gave tactful notice of her proximity.

'*Boa noite, querida*,' he said huskily, trailing his hand down Catherine's flushed cheek as he opened the door for her. 'Until tomorrow.'

She nodded wordlessly, then slid inside the strange room to lean against the door in the darkness, so shaken that it was some time before she could move. When she was recovered enough to turn on the lights in the strange room her eyes flew in dismay to her reflection in the gilded mirror on the far wall. For once she had cause to be grateful for Eduardo's high-handedness. Had she still shared a room with Ana, the latter would have known at a glance why Eduardo had taken so long to say goodnight.

CHAPTER SEVEN

NEXT morning over breakfast Eduardo asked if Catherine and Ana would accompany him to the airport to meet his great-aunt.

'Tia Clara will like a welcome from a fellow Inglesa,' agreed Ana. 'But I have much to see to this morning, Eduardo.' She smiled at him blandly. 'Perhaps you will not mind *too* much if Catherine goes alone with you to Oporto. There is nothing for her to do here.'

'Are you sure?' said Catherine doubtfully. 'You know I'm only too willing to do anything I can to help.'

'You can help with Tia Clara,' Ana informed her, making a face. 'She is elderly and very—how do you say?—outspoken? Also she will not speak a word of Portuguese, although I feel certain she is capable of doing so.'

'If she's English, how exactly is she related to you?' asked Catherine, intrigued.

'She is my mother's aunt,' explained Eduardo. 'You remember I spoke of English connections?'

Catherine nodded. 'Of course. She was the lady in Warwick you used to visit, Ana.'

Eduardo smiled at Catherine significantly. '*Entao*, Tia Clara is truly a tyrant! She is the only surviving daughter of a Midlands wine merchant. He traded much with Portugal, with the result that two of his daughters, one of them my grandmother, married

115

Portuguese husbands. Not so Tia Clara. She remained *solteira* all her life.'

'A fact which will not surprise you when you meet her!' laughed Ana.

In deference to the age of Eduardo's great-aunt Clara Catherine changed her jeans and T-shirt after breakfast for her white skirt and printed silk shirt, as more in keeping to greet a lady likely to be in an irascible mood after the flight—a form of transport she apparently detested.

'Frankly I think she's game to fly at all if she's as elderly as you say,' said Catherine as she hung up her clothes.

'We do not know her exact age,' chuckled Ana. 'She guards the secret fiercely. But we know she is in her late eighties. She is also very wealthy—but so fond of cats, she will probably leave all her money to a cats' home!'

'*Bom dia*,' said Eduardo, when Catherine joined him in the car.

She smiled at him. 'Good morning? Didn't we meet at breakfast?'

'*Pois é*. But not alone!' He smiled, raising her hand to his lips for an instant before returning both hands to the wheel to drive through the maze of cobbled streets on their way out of Pontalegre. 'You have changed your clothes, Catherine.'

'I thought your aunt might not approve of trousers.'

'It is difficult to anticipate Tia Clara's reaction to anything. Leonor and Cristina did not want Ana to invite her to the wedding, but Ana and I are fond of the old lady. I worry sometimes that she is lonely.'

'Does she live alone?'

'No. She has a companion. Tia Clara insists the unfortunate lady remains in Warwick to look after the cats.'

'Perhaps she's glad of the break from your aunt.'

'*Sem duvida!*'

They smiled at each other in undisguised delight at the pleasure of being alone together for a while. The day was sunny without being overhot, the sky was a brilliant blue, and Eduardo, in a lightweight fawn suit with a white shirt open at the neck, looked to Catherine like everything she had ever dreamed of in a man. He gave her a sidelong glance, colour rising in his taut face as he intercepted her look.

'Do not look at me so,' he ordered tersely.

Catherine's eyebrows rose in question.

'Because,' he continued, staring at the road, 'if you do I shall be forced to stop the car and make love to you here and now where all may see.'

She relaxed, grinning. 'Bad idea!'

'Why?' he demanded.

'There's a lot of traffic on the road. We might cause an accident.'

His face shadowed. 'God forbid!' He gave her a sidelong, narrowed glance. 'I thought you meant you did not wish me to make love to you.'

'Did you? Really?'

He breathed in deeply. 'All lovers have such doubts.'

'You're not my lover.'

'What am I, then?'

Catherine was silent. How would she describe Eduardo Barroso? One thing was certain. Whatever description she applied, her life was going to be horribly empty without him once she went back to

England. But she wasn't going to think about that. Not until she was forced to.

'Well?' he demanded. 'You have not answered me.'

'No, Eduardo, and I'm not going to.'

'You realise this may be the only time we shall be alone together today?'

'Perhaps it's just as well.'

'You do not like being with me like this?'

'You know perfectly well I like it! Far too much. To be honest I wish we could go on driving like this together indefinitely,' she admitted.

'Then stay after the wedding!' he said forcibly. 'We can drive together as much as we wish—I will even promise not to make love to you any more if this is what you fear.'

'Oh, Eduardo, I don't *fear* it at all! That's the problem.' Catherine sighed shakily. 'What happens between us is pretty frightening, just the same—totally outside my experience. I never imagined...' She trailed into silence.

'Nor I.' He reached out a hand to clasp hers so hard it hurt. 'Yet you wish to run away from me!'

'No, I don't, Eduardo, but I'm going home just the same.' She changed the subject firmly, talking about the scenery, the wedding, anything she could think of to bring them both down to earth.

For a time Eduardo's replies were monosyllabic, his face set, but gradually he responded, his occasional sidelong smile so possessive that Catherine was both glad and sorry when they reached the airport. To prolong their time alone together Eduardo had made no attempt to hurry on the journey, which meant a dash from the car when they arrived at the terminal building. Eduardo immediately spotted his aunt sailing through the crowd, followed by an airport attendant with a trolley containing her luggage. Pulling Catherine with him, he threaded his way quickly towards the upright figure which looked so ineluctably British in a tailored suit and felt hat, a light overcoat draped over one arm, the strap of her alligator handbag firmly hooked over the other.

'Eduardo!' The skilfully made-up face was lined with age, but bright with the intelligence of a still razor-sharp mind as she beamed at her great-nephew. He bent to kiss her hand then embraced her with sincere affection, kissing her on both cheeks.

'Tia Clara, you look wonderful!'

She held him away from her, examining his face with satisfaction. 'So do you, my boy—more like your father every day! Handsome devils, you Barrosos. Here,' she said briskly, 'give this lad a tip, would you? You might as well take charge of my luggage now you're here—and careful of that hatbox!'

'First allow me to present Ana's friend who is staying with us.' Eduardo turned to draw Catherine forward. 'Since Miss Ward is a fellow countrywoman of yours, she came with me to greet you.'

Clara Holroyd turned her attention from her luggage, her eyebrows shooting beneath the brim of her hat as she came face to face with Catherine, who braced herself, resigned. Isabel again, no doubt!

'How do you do?' she said, smiling politely. 'I'm Catherine Ward.'

'Ward?' barked Miss Holroyd, and peered more closely into Catherine's face. 'Have we met? I can't quite place it but you remind me of someone.'

Eduardo escorted them quickly to the car, explaining to his aunt how startling he'd found the resemblance himself at first. 'But as you get to know this charming young lady better,' he said firmly, 'you will find the resemblance fades.' He squeezed Catherine's hand swiftly as he handed her into the car.

As Eduardo drove off Clara Holroyd twisted round, shaking her head in wonder. 'Ana's friend, did you say, dear? You're not a relative of any kind?'

'No, Miss Holroyd. I shared a room with Ana when she came to take a course of business studies in London.'

'Catherine was very kind to Ana at the time of our great tragedy,' said Eduardo gravely. 'We are very happy for the opportunity to thank her in person at last.'

'Ah! So that's who you are.'

'If you look more closely,' went on Eduardo, meeting Catherine's eyes in the driving-mirror, 'you will see that Catherine resembles Isabel Cardoso.'

Miss Holroyd shook her head. 'It can't be that. I hardly knew the girl. Her father would never let her out of that convent to come and visit me.' She scrutinised Catherine closely. 'Maddening. I can't quite place it.'

'It must be Isabel you think of, Tia Clara,' insisted Eduardo. 'I remember her very clearly.'

'Well, I don't,' contradicted Miss Holroyd. 'Though I believe the child took after her mother for looks—— Wait a minute! That's it, of course. Now I come to think of it, Catherine reminds me a little of Bess. My sister Elizabeth.'

Catherine, faced with two ghosts instead of one, looked so dismayed that Eduardo suggested they stop for coffee.

'This is a splendid idea,' said Miss Holroyd, once they were seated in a pleasant roadside restaurant. 'Now then, young lady, I think there must be a Holroyd lurking on some branch of your family tree.'

Catherine shook her head, depressed. 'Not that I know of.'

'Who do you look like?'

'Far too many people for my taste!' returned Catherine tartly, and Miss Holroyd chuckled.

'*Touché*, Miss! I meant do you follow your father or your mother for looks?'

Catherine hesitated, flushing a little. 'From old photographs I look a little like my mother at the same age. My eyes are the same colour.'

Eduardo regarded her thoughtfully. 'Perhaps my aunt is right. There must be some link somewhere to explain the mystery.'

'Young Catherine might turn out to be your long-lost sister, Eduardo,' observed Miss Holroyd slyly, watching them.

'*Meu Deus*, I hope not!'

Miss Holroyd raised a quizzical eyebrow at him. 'Remembering your father's devotion to your mother, it's hardly likely is it, boy?' She turned to Catherine briskly. 'Now then, child, how far can you trace your family back?'

Catherine's face shuttered. 'No distance at all, I'm afraid. I wish I could. This haunted feeling gives me the creeps.'

Miss Holroyd gave a wicked little smile. 'I bet it does. Lord knows, I'd hate to think Bess had come back to haunt *me*.'

Eduardo shook his head, laughing as he helped her to her feet. 'Did you not care for your sister?'

'No, I didn't. I was very fond of Emily, *your* grand-mother, but Bess, quite frankly, was a right pain in the neck, always whingeing about her ailments. I think she only married José Cardoso because he was old enough to be her father. He spoiled her rotten.' Miss Holroyd gave a conspiratorial wink at Catherine as they got in the car. 'For years Bess used her delicate health to keep José from her bed, the fool. But he must have got there in the end. Bess fell pregnant in her forties and proved her delicacy beyond all question by dying in childbirth.'

'Poor lady,' said Catherine. 'You never knew your aunt, then, Eduardo?'

'Alas, no.'

'I'd forgotten that,' admitted Miss Holroyd. 'Anyway, Eduardo, it sounds as though Isabel took after her mother right enough. When you think she repaid your mother's kindness by drowning herself like that she must have been as much a pain in the neck as our Bess.'

Catherine choked on an involuntary gurgle as she met Eduardo's look of distaste in the driving-mirror.

'I am glad you find suicide so amusing,' he snapped, then eyed his aunt militantly. 'You are wrong, Tia. Isabel was not at all this pain in the neck of yours.'

'Of course she was, boy. Sensible girls don't go drowning themselves over a man.'

'True,' he agreed suavely, catching Catherine's eye. 'They travel the world instead.'

Catherine bit back an angry retort and lapsed into silence, leaving Miss Holroyd, apparently unaware that anything was amiss, to maintain the conver-sation with talk of the wedding for the rest of the journey to Pontalegre.

When they arrived at Casa das Camelias Catherine took care to jump from the car unaided, in no mood for the most fleeting of physical contact with Eduardo. 'I'll see your aunt to her room if you have things to do,' she told Eduardo.

'Nothing is more important than assuring my guests' comfort,' he said coldly. 'Come in, Tia Clara, you must be tired.'

'Nonsense, boy.' Miss Holroyd walked erect across the cool hall, her face lighting up as Ana came racing down the stairs to hug her. 'Careful, careful, you hoyden, you'll break a leg. Your young man will require you in good working order tomorrow, remember.'

'Tia Clara!' Ana hugged her, bombarding her great-aunt with questions, breaking off belatedly to tell Eduardo that friends of his were in the small *sala*, waiting for him.

Miss Holroyd waved Eduardo away briskly. 'Don't hang about for my sake, Eduardo. Thank you for meeting me, boy, you're excused now. Off you go.'

The 'boy' inclined his handsome head, informed his aunt that he would bring her luggage later, and, ignoring Catherine completely, went off to seek out his guests.

'Is he in a bad mood *again*?' whispered Ana as they escorted Miss Holroyd to the large, beautiful bedroom at the far end of the house.

'Catherine laughed in the wrong place, that's all,' said her great-aunt cheerfully. 'Fatal. Men detest it—which is why I never married one of them.'

Catherine left Miss Holroyd with Ana, then went off to tidy up after the hot journey. As she washed her face she eyed herself moodily, consoling herself that, however much she resembled the two Cardoso women physically, otherwise she was chalk to their cheese. So instead of behaving like the proverbial pain in the neck, she told her reflection crossly, you just tootle off back home on Saturday as planned, Catherine Ward.

By the time the company assembled for lunch Eduardo had regained his normal good humour. At first the conversation was general, the wedding the main topic, but when Eduardo became embroiled in a heated discussion with Ana his aunt turned to Catherine with a smile.

'How do you like Portugal, Miss Ward?'

'Very much indeed. I've been to Lisbon several times, but this is my first visit to the Minho.'

'It's very picturesque here, I admit, but rather quiet for some tastes.'

'Not to me.' Catherine smiled. 'I was brought up in a small English village. Pontalegre is a city by comparison.'

'Yet Ana tells me you've been travelling the world in a cruise liner.' Miss Holroyd helped herself to cheese. 'What's your job now?'

'I haven't got one yet. When I go home at the end of the week I start job-hunting in earnest. Something on the administrative side of travel, preferably. Most of my friends live in London so I'll probably end up there.'

'Even though you prefer the country?'

Catherine nodded, resigned. 'I'm more likely to get a job in London, so I don't have much choice.'

Miss Holroyd eyed her thoughtfully for a moment, then turned to Eduardo. 'If you're in such crying need of help with this *Turismo de Habitação* of yours,

Eduardo, why haven't you thought of asking Catherine to take Ana's place?'

Ana clapped her hands, beaming. 'But of course. How clever you are, Tia. That would be perfect!'

'Not really.' Catherine felt her cheeks grow hot as Eduardo, a startled look in his eyes, failed to join in the general chorus of approval. 'I wouldn't be much use. I can't speak Portuguese.'

Eduardo eyed her expressionlessly. '*Não faz mal*— I could teach you. You are right, *sem duvida*, Tia. Why did I not think of that?'

'Your legal brain is rusty, boy,' teased his aunt. 'Too full of tourists and vines and so on, these days. If you ask me, Eduardo, I think it would be ideal to have someone like Catherine to deal with your tourists. Ana tells me the majority of them are British, or at least English-speaking.'

'No, really!' Catherine shook her head. 'It's not possible.'

'Why not?' demanded Miss Holroyd. 'You need a job, Eduardo needs someone to help him. You've had the same training as Ana, so where's the problem?'

The problem, thought Catherine, was that Eduardo seemed a shade unenthusiastic for a man who only this morning had been so pressing for her to stay.

'At least give it some thought, Catherine,' urged Ana. 'You have all the necessary skills. You would soon learn Portuguese to manage.'

'Do not rush her,' commanded Eduardo, then turned to look at Catherine. 'Perhaps after dinner tonight you might spare me a few moments to discuss so interesting a proposition.'

Catherine nodded coolly. 'We can discuss it, certainly.'

Clara Holroyd looked pleased with herself. 'Splendid! Now, Ana, I know I'm ancient, but I'm not entirely useless—yet. If there's anything I can do to help just say the word.'

There was no lack of employment for anyone at the Casa das Camelias that day. From early afternoon onward the young maids were kept busy in merely answering the clang of the great iron bell on the street door, as wedding gifts arrived, and visitors came to drink wine, or coffee, and give their best wishes to the bride. Later on the caterers arrived with tables for the wedding feast, which sparked off much heated discussion as to the best location for everything as Ana directed operations to ensure sufficient space for the dancing at her Minhota wedding.

Catherine saw very little of Eduardo as she helped Miss Holroyd list the wedding presents as they arrived, then flew to the rescue when an overwrought Ana cried a little because the floral decorations delivered for the buffet tables were not to her taste. Catherine drove her at once to the market, where they bought every blossom available, then rushed back with their spoils to the house, vying with each other in cheerful rivalry to transform the decorations to works of art which met at last with Ana's approval.

After dinner that night Eduardo sent Ana to bed early.

'I will not keep Catherine talking long, *carinha*,' he said, kissing her.

'I shall retire myself,' declared Miss Holroyd. She extended her cheek to Eduardo and Catherine for a kiss, then went off with Ana, one eyelid lowered in an unmistakable wink at Catherine as she made her exit.

The small *sala* was very quiet as Eduardo strolled across the room to a tray of decanters, his manner making it very clear that his present role was purely that of prospective employer, and nothing to do with the would-be lover of the night before.

'You're still angry because I laughed at Isabel,' blurted Catherine, taking the war into the enemy's camp.

Eduardo glanced up from the port he was pouring. 'No. Nor at this moment do I wish to discuss my unfortunate cousin. We are here to assess your suitability to take Ana's place.'

Rebuffed, Catherine waved away the glass of port he offered. The word 'suitability', even allowing for Eduardo's sometimes pedantic choice of vocabulary, was oddly pejorative. 'The idea was none of mine,' she pointed out.

'No. Nevertheless it is an excellent one, you must agree.' He drank some of his own wine unhurriedly. 'I need someone to work for me. You need a job. You have travelled widely, therefore have no qualms about working far from home, *não é*?'

Since all of this was irrefutable Catherine made no comment.

Eduardo eyed her quizzically. 'Have you nothing to say?'

She shrugged. 'My lack of Portuguese would be a handicap.'

'Only a little, and only at first. You would soon learn.' He sat down on a straight chair at the table. 'We have not discussed a salary, of course. I could possibly pay you a little more than Ana.' He thought for a moment then named a sum in *escudos*. 'This would not be enough?' he asked as she silently converted it to sterling.

'More than enough. Since board and lodging go with the job it's very generous.'

'Then you will take the job?' he said swiftly.

Catherine got up. 'No. Definitely not.'

Eduardo leapt to his feet, scowling. *'Porquê?'*

Her chin lifted. 'Because the idea of my working for you never entered your head until Miss Holroyd suggested it——'

'You are refusing just because the idea was hers and not mine?' he demanded furiously, all his detachment suddenly vanished.

'Since you mention it, yes.'

'I do not understand!'

'When everyone else thought it was so perfect for me to take Ana's place your manners wouldn't allow you to say you—you didn't want me.'

Eduardo tossed back the remainder of his port and set the glass down with a crack on the table. 'And if I tell you that I do want you?' he demanded, eyes glittering.

Catherine tensed, backing away involuntarily as he jumped up to stride towards her.

'Deus me livre!' he said violently. 'You must know I want you, Catherine. You lie if you deny it. The torment of it is affecting my entire personality! I am not normally so moody, so easy to anger. Yet today I felt murderous merely because you laughed at my aunt's remark about Isabel.'

'I didn't *mean* to laugh. Blame your aunt's sense of humour—you said you liked that in a woman!'

His face relaxed slightly. 'And so I do. But for a moment it was as though you were mocking my boyhood worship of Isabel.'

'I'd be the last one to do that.' She met his eyes squarely. 'In a way I can understand what drove Isabel to do what she did. My way of dealing with rejection was different, that's all.'

'Your way was preferable, Catherine.'

'Ah, yes, but I realise now that what I felt for Dan was nothing——' She stopped dead, blushing vividly.

Eduardo's eyes narrowed in speculation, riveted to the tide of colour as it ebbed from her face.

'Catherine, let us resume this conversation after the wedding,' he said slowly at last. 'In the meantime, do not refuse the job without more thought. Since you insist we must take time to know each other, how better to do so?' He smiled persuasively. 'It is not late. Ring your mother now, if you wish, to ask her approval. Perhaps you might also question her about your family tree, if only to satisfy Tia Clara's curiosity.'

Catherine stiffened. 'I can't ring my mother right now because she's on her way to join the ship for a Caribbean cruise. Mr Carfax persuaded her to accompany him on holiday for once, so I negotiated a good deal on some passages before I left my job on the liner.' She looked away, her heart like a lump of ice in her chest. 'There wouldn't be any point in discussing my family tree with her anyway, Eduardo. There's something I haven't told you.'

His eyes narrowed at her tone. 'It is unpleasant, this something?'

'It depends on your point of view, I suppose.' She took in a deep breath, and turned to face him. 'Actually, I do know something of my family tree. Enough to keep it strictly to myself. I've never even told Ana.'

He frowned. 'Told her what, Catherine? I do not understand.'

'That my mother's name is the same as mine—Ward. In words of one syllable, Eduardo,' she added doggedly, 'I'm a product of one of those one-parent families all too common in the UK these days. I've no idea who my father is. All my mother would tell me, once I was old enough to know, was that she once had a brief love-affair, I was the result, and there was never any question of marriage. All I know is that he was young—so much younger than my mother that she never even told him she was pregnant.'

'*Meu Deus*!' Eduardo sat beside her, taking her cold hands in his. 'She must be a brave lady, your mother.'

Catherine nodded, her eyes fixed on their intertwined fingers. 'She is.'

'You grew up in the home of your grandparents, then?'

'No. When my mother refused to have me adopted they washed their hands of her.'

Eduardo stared down at her in horror. 'They wished to part your mother from her child?'

'They said it was for the best. Which of course it was—for them. My mother wouldn't hear of it. You see she was no young, biddable girl. She was a woman in her thirties, and assistant matron at a boys' public school. Which made the shame even worse for my grandparents. Old enough to know better, and all that.'

'So what did your mother do?'

'She worked a term's notice at the school, utilising the time to find the kind of job possible for someone in her awkward situation.' Catherine looked away. 'After a lot of searching she did. Once I'd arrived my mother became housekeeper to a widower who made no objection to my presence as long as the quiet of his household was never disrupted. She's been there ever since. So have I, more or less. Mr Carfax is a retired barrister, and a dear. If he'd had his way I think he'd have married Mother years ago.'

Eduardo shook his head, his brow furrowed. 'It is a very sad story. And your grandparents? Did they relent?'

'No.' Catherine's mouth tightened. 'I never even met them. They died when I was a child.'

Eduardo was silent for some time, his face thoughtful. After a while Catherine tried to withdraw her hands, but his grasp tightened.

'Catherine,' he began after a while, 'I am honoured by your confidence, but why was it vital for *me* to know this so sad little story, if you never discuss it?'

'Because I'm afraid you see the job here as a way for us to become lovers,' said Catherine bluntly. 'So I'm turning your offer down. Heaven knows I'd love the job. But if—if I stay the inevitable would happen. I admit it. So I'm going back where I belong. My mother had a lover who spoiled her for everyone else, and wrecked her life. I don't intend the same thing to happen to me, Eduardo. Ever.'

The colour drained from his face. 'But you have had a lover, nevertheless!' he taunted bitterly.

She shook her head. 'You're wrong. Dan was just a boyfriend. I know now that what he and I had together was just boy-and-girl stuff. Besides, I thought of Dan as a prospective husband, remember. Which is the difference. You're definitely not husband material, Eduardo Barroso. At least not for me.'

'You would not desire me for a husband?' he demanded, incensed.

'I didn't *say* that,' she said desperately. 'But can you imagine anything less likely?'

'*Porquê*?'

'You know exactly why. You've got a pedigree a mile long, while I don't even know who my father was!' Catherine swallowed hard. 'I'll never know either, because if I bring the subject up my mother flatly refuses to discuss it, other than to say that I have nothing to be ashamed of, but that he was just too young for her.'

'Yet he cannot have been a mere ordinary boy, Catherine,' said Eduardo decisively. 'Otherwise why, after knowing him, has she never looked at another man?'

'I don't know, I don't know!'

Eduardo rose, holding out his hand to her. 'Come. Do not distress yourself, *carinha*. I think it is time you sought your bed. Tomorrow will be a tiring day. We shall defer this conversation until after the wedding.' When she put her hand in his he drew her up gently until she was in his arms, his eyes locked with hers. '*I* care nothing for your ancestry, Catherine. Any man would be proud to be your father, while I——' He paused, his eyes narrowed to a sudden heated glitter. 'While I, *querida*, would be proud to play whatever part in your life you wish.' He bent his head to hers, and, telling herself this must be positively the last time, Catherine gave herself up to his kiss.

But the kiss, delicate and caressing at first, all too swiftly metamorphosed into a heated, mutual frenzy, so overpowering that it took every last ounce of willpower Catherine possessed to push Eduardo away at last, her resolve hardening as she faced the unpalatable truth. The only course open to her, it was increasingly obvious, was to remove herself from temptation in the person of Eduardo Barroso the moment she could decently take her leave after Ana's wedding.

CHAPTER EIGHT

THE day of the wedding dawned sunny and cloudless, just as Ana had predicted, and from first opening her eyes on it Catherine had no time for brooding. Ana, bright and early in true bridal tradition, tapped on the door shortly after Catherine woke, a beaming maid hard on her heels with a laden tray.

'Forgive me for disturbing you so early, *querida*, but I thought we could share breakfast here in your new room.' Ana perched herself cross-legged on the other bed. 'Then my wedding dress will not suffer from smears of *marmelada*!'

Catherine laughed, relieved that she wasn't required to face Eduardo over the breakfast table. Today was Ana's day, and nothing must be allowed to spoil it. Ana, however, was by no means too wrapped up in her own happiness to drop the subject of Catherine as her own replacement.

'Did Eduardo not charm you into agreement last night?' she demanded, and smiled wickedly. 'Most women find it easy to say yes to him!'

'I'm sure they do,' said Catherine drily, feeling it was hardly the moment to inform Ana that she had no intention of working for Eduardo. 'But it's not something I can rush into.'

'*Pois é*. You will naturally wish to talk to your mother,' agreed Ana. 'Now, what would you like to eat? Elsa has provided a feast!'

Ana's sisters and their families arrived straight after breakfast, joined shortly afterwards by the da Cunha ménage, the younger girls in such a high state of excitement that the house soon began to sound like a gigantic aviary, the shrill young voices echoing through the ancient rooms as preparations for the great event got under way.

Miss Holroyd, enthroned on a sofa in the main *sala* out of harm's way, looked on in enjoyment through the open doors as a tide of bridal excitement ebbed and flowed along the corridor. Eduardo, she informed Catherine at one stage, was in the garden with the rest of the men, safe out of harm's way with their cigars, drinking coffee under the camellias.

'Why don't you join them for a while, dear?' she suggested.

'I'd rather join you if you don't mind, Miss Holroyd,' said Catherine. 'The hairdresser's arrived to do Ana's hair, so I'm superfluous to requirements for the moment.'

'Then come and sit here for a moment and share the coffee Elsa has brought me,' she commanded.

Catherine was glad of the chance to relax for a moment away from the general hubbub, which, because most of it was a flood of excited Portuguese, was becoming rather a strain.

'You look tired, my dear,' observed Miss Holroyd.

Catherine smiled. 'Ana was awake at the crack of dawn. I only hope she lasts the course today.'

'I'm sure bridal adrenalin will keep her ticking over. Besides,' added Miss Holroyd with a sigh, 'she's very young. You girls should be brimming with energy at your age. Ah, here comes Eduardo.'

Her great-nephew came swiftly across the large, formal *sala de visitas* to greet them. He kissed his aunt's cheek, giving Catherine a smile which lingered a moment as he met her eyes, then he moved away to sit on a pale green velvet love-seat the other side of Miss Holroyd, as though removing himself from a danger zone. He gestured at the sunshine outside. 'Ana's prayers were answered. The day is beautiful, *não é*?'

Miss Holroyd chuckled. 'How Anglicised you are, Eduardo! I thought it was only the British who discussed the weather *ad nauseam*.'

'It must be in his genes,' said Catherine lightly.

'*Sem duvida*,' he agreed, looking at her. 'They give us much in common, Catherine.'

'That reminds me,' said Miss Holroyd. 'Did you manage to persuade her to take the job, Eduardo?'

'I promised to think about it,' said Catherine swiftly, which was no lie. Her mind had been occupied with the subject most of the night.

'Good girl,' said Miss Holroyd approvingly. 'No point in acting on impulse.'

'*E verdade*,' said Eduardo with a hint of bitterness. 'Catherine, alas, was not infected by your enthusiasm on the subject, Tia.'

'You mean she didn't say yes at the drop of a hat!' Miss Holroyd smiled in amusement. 'A refreshing change. I don't suppose many people say no to you, Eduardo.'

He made a brief dismissive gesture. 'Probably because I try to ask the right questions. Now, let us think of other things.'

'Like weddings,' said Catherine lightly as she jumped up. 'I'd better see how the bride's hair is progressing.'

From then on the day became a blur of feverish activity and gaiety as Catherine set to work to help Ana dress. First there were the knitted white stockings and small black clogs, then layers of stiff petticoats before the beautiful, rather barbaric dress was taken from its shroud of white cotton. When the last finishing touch had finally been made Ana, radiant with her hair piled high beneath a small veil of priceless old lace, looked like a ravishingly pretty doll in her gold-encrusted black velvet. Gold chains borrowed from every member of the family hung round her neck in profusion, mingling with as many gold brooches as Leonor and Cristina could pin to the bodice. As the crowning touch Carlos's present to his bride was fastened round Ana's neck—an exquisite gold filigree heart on the heaviest gold chain of the entire collection.

Catherine stood back, joining with Leonor and Cristina in heartfelt admiration of the completed picture, before the other two hurried off to join their families.

'You look gorgeous, Ana Barroso,' she said, smiling. 'You do your bridegroom proud!'

'*Obrigada, querida*!' Ana kissed her swiftly on both cheeks, then gave her a hug. 'Now hurry, Catherine. You must get ready yourself.'

'I won't take long, I promise. By the time the photographer's managed to keep all your bridesmaids still for the wedding pictures I'll be there.' Catherine smiled, a sudden lump in her throat. 'Be happy, Ana.'

She sniffed inelegantly. 'Here—you've forgotten your flowers.'

Ana's face was pensive as she gathered up the posy of flowers wreathed in traditional style round a carved candle. 'There may be no other chance to say this, Catherine. But, now we have come together again, do not let my marriage separate us. Promise you will come to stay with Carlos and me soon at Quinta da Floresta?'

Catherine nodded briskly as she pushed Ana towards the door. 'Of course I will. Now off you go. Everyone's waiting.'

As cries of appreciation greeted Ana from the bevy of bridesmaids and female relatives waiting outside in the corridor Catherine made for her own room, bent on achieving an elegance at least some way comparable with Ana's sisters. After paying swift, careful attention to her face she brushed her heavy mass of hair up high on her head and secured it in a knot, then put on a severely plain ivory silk suit which had been her final purchase at the liner's boutique. She threaded her own pearl drops in her ears, added a single string of large baroque pearls borrowed from her mother, then adjusted her deep-crowned ivory silk hat so that its outsize bow trimming sat dead centre above the brim she tilted low over her eyes.

'You'll do,' she told her reflection as she pulled on her gloves. She picked up her small purse, squared her shoulders, then left the room to head for the laughter and voices coming from the *sala de visitas*, just as Fernanda, resplendent in her best black, came marching along the corridor to fetch her.

'Dona Caterina, *que beleza!*' she exclaimed. 'You look like a bride yourself!'

The words speared Catherine with such a secret pang that it took effort to summon up a laughing response as she hurried with Fernanda towards the *sala de visitas*. They paused outside the open double doors, unseen for a moment as Catherine gazed on the scene the photographer had obviously just posed. Eduardo, spectacularly handsome in formal dark morning dress, stood before the great fireplace with a laughing Ana on his arm, flanked by the troupe of bridesmaids, ranging from Maria Luisa da Cunha, aged eighteen, to little five-year-old Emilia Nogeira, each one a replica of the bride right down to the beaming smile.

As Eduardo caught sight of Catherine his eyes lit up at the precise point when the photographer took the shot to preserve the moment for posterity. Then the new arrival was spotted and welcomed into the animated, elegantly dressed throng of Barroso relatives and friends. To Catherine's dismay Ana insisted she pose with her for a photograph, then for a second with Eduardo to complete the trio before Elsa arrived to announce that the first of the cars had arrived to transport the guests to the church.

In the ensuing confusion no one noticed when Eduardo drew Catherine aside for a fleeting, private moment.

'You are so beautiful you take the breath away, Catherine.'

'So are you.' She turned away blindly as Miss Holroyd sailed towards her, majestic in grey moire and violet-trimmed hat.

'We shall be travelling together,' she announced. 'Are you all right, Catherine? You look very fetching, but rather pale.'

'Reflection from my hat—I'm fine,' Catherine assured her.

'Not that I'm surprised you're tired. I imagine getting Ana ready on time was no mean feat!'

Ana's wedding day was a uniquely poignant experience to Catherine from start to finish, not least because during the long nuptial mass before the great gilded altar of the Igreja Matriz she found herself not only deeply moved by the ceremony, but also utterly convinced that after knowing Eduardo it would be impossible to make vows of this kind to any other man.

At Ana's behest, instead of driving back to the Casa das Camelias by car, the bride and groom and their attendants walked through the town in procession, the bridesmaids with hands on hips in approved Minhota style. Smiles shone on every face, Carlos da Cunha's grin of triumph reflected in his bride's radiance as people leaned out of windows and thronged pavements to shower blessings on the happy couple as the procession passed, while Catherine, leaving Miss Holroyd to ride home with Eduardo, took photographs at every possible juncture along the way to Casa das Camelias, including the scene in the courtyard, which Elsa and the maids had transformed into a veritable bridal bower. In addition to the table arrangements Ana and Catherine had doctored there were flowers entwined in the iron rings where horses had once been tethered, more among the creeper and in tubs along the walls, the perfume joining with the laughter in the air as the bride and groom received kisses and congratulations from their guests, to the accompaniment of flashing cameras and popping champagne corks.

'You are enjoying Ana's Minhota wedding, Catherine?' asked Eduardo later, once he was free to mingle with his guests.

She smiled at him brightly. 'How could I not? It's wonderful. All weddings should be like this.'

Their eyes locked, their polite social smiles fading, and it was Catherine who looked away first, as the sound of fifes and accordians heralded the arrival of the musicians to play for the country dances Ana loved so much.

Due to the strain of her emotions Catherine's solitary glass of champagne went straight to her head, and after a while, seeing that other ladies were doing the same, she went upstairs to take off her hat and brush out her hair. Afterwards she returned to join the group clustered round Miss Holroyd to watch the dancers take their places. In the twilight the golden globes of light in the camellia trees provided an enchanted backdrop for flashing dark eyes and white smiles as Carlos da Cunha and his bride, the former in his black velvet suit and embroidered white shirt, Ana in all her gold-encrusted glory, led the couples in the lively dance that Catherine learned was the *vira*. She felt wistful as she watched Eduardo take Maria Luisa da Cunha's hand to join his sister and her new husband, his formal wedding garb no whit incongruous alongside the traditional Minhota costume of his partner. The shrill music beat out a lively rhythm for the quick-stepping dance which consisted of a fixed set of patterns as the dancers whirled and weaved in and out, Eduardo performing the complicated steps with an athletic grace which outshone every other man present, to Catherine's biased eyes. There were exchanges of partners as the *vira* gave way to the *chula*, then to the *caminha verde* and the *malhão*. Leonor and Cristina were drawn, laughing, into the dance after a while, but not even the most eager beseeching of some of the young male guests persuaded Catherine to follow suit.

'I'd never get the hang of it,' she confided to Miss Holroyd. 'I'd probably fall flat on my face.'

'I admit I'd rather an old-fashioned waltz, myself!' agreed the old lady, chuckling.

Eduardo materialised out of the dusk to sit beside them, declaring he needed a rest to regain his breath. 'If I request a waltz, would you dance with me, Tia Clara?' he demanded.

'Certainly not. At my age a broken leg is catastrophe.' Miss Holroyd smiled wickedly. 'But Catherine might, if you ask her nicely.'

'No!' Catherine blurted, then smiled, embarrassed. 'I mean, I've got two left feet when I waltz.'

Eduardo looked sceptical as Ana came running up, hand in hand with Carlos, breathless and laughing as she accused Catherine of laziness.

'Why will you not join in? When we were in college you would dance all night!'

'She *says* she has two left feet,' observed Eduardo.

'Perhaps we are too rustic for you, Catherine,' teased Carlos.

'Too skilful! You're all so expert at these dances, I wouldn't dare make a fool of myself.' She glanced across the crowded courtyard. 'Have the musicians finished already?'

'No,' said Eduardo. 'They will retire to the kitchen for refreshment, and in the meantime we shall have some recorded music until they return.'

As he spoke the strains of a dreamy modern waltz drifted from the loudspeakers hidden under the colonnade, and he turned to Miss Holroyd with a ceremonious bow.

'Will you not dance with me just once, Tia Clara? I promise you shall not break a leg.'

Giving in to the urgings of the others, Miss Holroyd allowed her great-nephew to guide her round the space rapidly cleared by the other guests as they saw Eduardo take to the floor with his elderly, but surprisingly agile partner. Ana sat down in her aunt's place beside Catherine, glad to rest a while after the hour of continuous dancing.

'I am glad you took off your hat,' she said. 'You could not dance with it on, beautiful though it is.'

'I don't intend to dance!'

'*Bobagem*!' scolded Ana. 'You know you love to. Please, *querida*. You must dance at my wedding to wish me the good luck.'

Catherine smiled, resigned. 'Oh, all right. But to this music only—if I'm asked, of course.'

'*If* you're asked!' Ana hooted with laughter.

'What is so amusing?' queried Eduardo, as he brought his aunt back to the applauding group.

'Catherine has agreed to dance at my wedding only while this type of music plays,' explained Ana, 'but worries she may lack a partner!'

There was a general burst of laughter as Catherine was besieged by a sudden rush of partners only too eager to take her out on the floor. Her dilemma was solved very neatly as, without a word, Eduardo calmly took her from under several indignant male noses to lead her into the waltz, Catherine not in the least surprised to find that he danced it as expertly as the *vira* and *chula* of his place of birth.

They revolved together in silence for some time, Eduardo's hold so correct that no one looking on would have guessed that the slight physical proximity allowed by the dance was a bitter-sweet agony for both of them from the moment they took the floor.

'You lied,' he said in a stifled voice at last. 'You waltz to perfection.'

'Only because I'm dancing with you,' she whispered, almost overpowered by the delight of being in his arms again.

Eduardo breathed in sharply. 'We move as one——' He broke off, his hand suddenly crushing hers. '*Deus*, Catherine—can you not believe that what you told me last night matters nothing to me?'

'It does to me!'

'I care nothing for your ancestry. All I want in life is to hold you in my arms like this forever, *querida*.'

'Don't—please! Take me back to the others.'

Eduardo said something unintelligible and violent in his own tongue, then led her back to the group around Miss Holroyd, where Catherine was given no mercy for the next hour, obliged to dance with every man who asked her until the recorded music gave way at last to the shrill sounds of the local musicians, allowing her to escape from the floor.

Catherine sank into a chair alongside Clara Holroyd, steeling herself to the prospect of having to watch Eduardo dancing with other women for the rest of the night. But to her surprise this was one ordeal spared her, since he promptly took the vacant chair beside her, announcing his duty was done.

'You mustn't feel obliged to stay with us, Eduardo,' said his great-aunt, eyes twinkling. 'Catherine and I will do very well together.'

'*Sem duvida*,' he agreed, smiling a little. 'Nevertheless have mercy on me, Tia. I have no wish to dance any more.'

'No more waltzes?'

He shook his head. 'There will be just another hour of all this *barulho*, then Ana must change for the drive to the Quinta da Floresta.'

The da Cunha family were booked into the Albergaria in the town, Catherine knew, leaving the bridal pair to the privacy of their future home for their wedding night. She felt a fierce pang of envy suddenly, thinking how wonderful it would be to steal away with Eduardo and live happy ever after too, just like Ana and Carlos.

'You're very quiet,' commented Miss Holroyd.

'Ana has worn her out.' Eduardo smiled a little at Catherine. 'In the morning you must sleep late. No one will disturb you until you are ready to face the day.'

Catherine returned the smile with effort. 'Tempting idea. I might do that. I need a breather before my travels on Saturday.'

Miss Holroyd expressed her displeasure at parting with Catherine so soon, and pressed her to make a visit to Warwick when she was back in England. Touched, Catherine accepted warmly, then got up in response to Ana's beckoning hand.

'Carlos will wait no longer,' announced the blushing bride, laughing. 'I am commanded to change, and wish Catherine to help me.'

Ana was jubilant as she divested herself of her gold chains and black velvet, demanding Catherine's opinion of her Minhota wedding, pleased when her friend assured her that the day had been a triumph from beginning to end.

'I'll send you the photographs I took,' Catherine promised her as she helped Ana change into a pink linen dress. 'You looked so lovely, Ana.'

Carefully Ana removed the carved candle from the heart of her bouquet and put it in her handbag. 'I shall keep this always,' she said, sighing happily. She hugged Catherine hard. 'It has been so good to have you here. Come back soon, *querida*.'

Catherine kissed her lovingly. 'Thank you for inviting me. It's been a—a wonderful experience. Now on your way, Senhora da Cunha, or Carlos will be galloping up here to throw you over his shoulder.'

Ana giggled as they hurried along the corridor together. 'It is only right that he should be impatient!' She stopped halfway along the corridor. 'Ah! I forgot. Go down and join the others in the hall, Catherine. I will be a moment only.'

Catherine gave her a last kiss then went through the double doors and on down the granite stairs to join the crowd of wedding guests milling below in the great hall.

'Is she not ready *yet*?' groaned Carlos.

'She's on her way,' Catherine assured him as she joined Miss Holroyd and Eduardo, and a moment later Ana appeared on the landing, her bouquet held high in the air.

'*Pronto*!' she cried, and tossed the flowers straight at Catherine, who caught them by pure reflex action, her colour high as Leonor and Cristina clapped their hands, laughing, among the cheers from the others.

Then Carlos bounded up the stairs to take his bride by the hand to rush her down to the square outside where his car waited, all the guests streaming out into the *praca* after them to speed the happy couple on their way into the moonlit night, before taking their leave in turn with much kissing and embracing and congratulations to Eduardo on the success of the day.

CHAPTER NINE

WHEN even Cristina and Leonor had finally been torn away by their husbands, and peace reigned at last at the Casa das Camelias, Elsa appeared to ask what refreshments were required now everyone was gone.

'A cup of tea would be very welcome,' said Miss Holroyd, who was looking every year of her uncertain age by this time. 'And I think Catherine should have something to eat. To my knowledge she's had nothing worth mentioning all day.'

In vain Catherine protested that she wasn't hungry. In minutes a tray of tea and coffee appeared in the small *sala*, complete with dainty, freshly cut sandwiches and a plate of the inevitable hot buttered toast.

Miss Holroyd chuckled. 'There, Catherine. An offer you can't refuse!'

It was oddly cosy to sit in the small *sala* together in the now silent house. Catherine nibbled on a slice of toast and drank the welcome tea, feeling strangely numb, anaesthetised for the moment from the pain of her forthcoming parting from Eduardo.

'So what's your final verdict on a Minhota wedding?' asked Miss Holroyd, shaking Catherine from her abstraction.

'It was utterly charming.' Catherine smiled a little. 'It's hard to imagine a lovelier—or happier—bride than Ana.'

'You'll be lonely from now on, Eduardo,' commented his great-aunt.

148

'*E verdade*,' he said, shooting a sombre look at Catherine.

'Which reminds me,' said Miss Holroyd. 'Have you decided yet about Eduardo's job? Will you take it?'

Catherine put down her cup with care. 'No, I'm afraid not. It—it isn't practicable.'

Miss Holroyd frowned. 'Why?'

'Catherine has no wish to leave England again so soon,' intervened Eduardo swiftly.

Miss Holroyd frowned. 'Rather a shame—I thought I'd been so clever, too.'

'And so you were,' said Eduardo with a wry smile. 'But for Catherine it was not the answer to my problem, *infelizmente*.'

'Oh, well, it's Catherine's decision—pity, though.' Miss Holroyd rose to her feet. 'I feel decidedly weary. If you'll take me along to my room, Eduardo, perhaps Catherine won't mind washing these dishes, since you've sent Elsa and the maids to bed.'

'This is not necessary——' began Eduardo stiffly, but Miss Holroyd flapped a hand at him.

'Nonsense. Catherine will be only too pleased, won't you, dear?'

'Of course.' Catherine rose to her feet, well aware that she was being manipulated.

'But you are tired, also,' objected Eduardo.

'Not too tired to save Elsa facing these dishes in the morning.'

'Then I shall help.'

'Well done,' approved Miss Holroyd. 'Do you good to experience life in your own kitchen. Goodnight, child.' She kissed Catherine's cheek, then took Eduardo's proffered arm, for once, it was plain, glad of its support.

Eduardo returned to the *sala* just as Catherine finished stacking the tray ready to carry to the kitchen.

'I apologise,' he said stiffly. 'You realise that my great-aunt believes she is doing us a great favour? My feelings, it is obvious, were not hidden as well as I would have wished.'

Catherine refused to look at him as he took the loaded tray from her. 'I'm surprised she's so keen to throw us together.'

Eduardo led the way into the kitchen, looking so incongruous with a tray in his hands that Catherine found she could actually manage a smile. He put down the tray with a clash of china and turned to Catherine with a sardonic smile.

'She disapproves of Antonia. Not that she has reason. Antonia and I have never been lovers, you understand.'

'Really?' Catherine found that her hands were shaking as she loaded china into one of the kitchen sinks. 'Not that it matters. Now.' She began washing cups and plates at top speed.

'You mean you do not care!'

'No,' she choked. 'I mean I *mustn't* care.' She dashed away a tear with a soapy hand, and with a curse Eduardo pulled her against him, turning her in his arms until her face rested against his chest.

'*Meu amor*, do not cry!' he implored.

Catherine sniffed inelegantly, and pulled away. 'No. All right.' Her smile died abruptly as she met the burning frustration in his eyes. 'Please! Don't look like that. We've known each other so short a time——'

'It makes no difference, Catherine.' He touched a hand to her cheek. 'Hours, days, minutes, *n'importa*.

I love you. Believe me, Catherine. If I never see you again in my entire life it will not change the way I feel for you, *querida*. I care nothing for the identity of your father. It is you that I want. Only you.'

All the colour drained from Catherine's face. She bit hard into her quivering lower lip, then turned back to the sink, fighting to control herself as she finished her task.

In silence Eduardo watched her until she'd washed the last item, standing with his arms folded as if to prevent himself from seizing her, and at last, in reasonable command of herself once more, Catherine turned to him with a determined smile.

'Aren't you going to dry the dishes?'

He stared at her blankly. '*Como*?'

'The dishes,' she repeated. 'Where are the towels to dry them?'

'I am contemplating the desert of my life without you and all you can speak of is dishes?' he demanded, something in his tone reassuring her that he was in command of himself again.

'I think we'd better just leave them to drain,' she said prosaically.

Eduardo said something extremely rude and idiomatic in English about the dishes, then took Catherine by the hand and led her from the kitchen.

'I'm sure you didn't learn that from your Dona Laura!' she said, trying to smile.

'No. There were English students at Coimbra.'

They faced each other in the *sala*, Catherine's face as pale as her suit.

'I'll say goodnight, then,' she said unsteadily.

Eduardo's jaw clenched, then, without warning, jerked her against him, crushing her so close that Catherine struggled wildly.

'No!' she gasped, but Eduardo merely turned her in his arms, holding her tightly as he looked over her shoulder at their reflection in the mirror above the fireplace.

'Yes, Catherine, yes!' he contradicted, his breath hot against her cheeks as he leaned closer. 'Look. Can you deny how right we look together?'

Catherine stared at their reflection, her heart hammering as she met the blaze in Eduardo's eyes. She could feel herself weakening, prepared to listen to an inner voice which argued that, if Eduardo was indifferent to her lack of pedigree, what point was there in ruining her life—and his, if he was to be believed—for the sake of some noble, quixotic notion about her origins? Sensing her capitulation, Eduardo's arms tightened triumphantly, his mouth seeking the hollow of her neck with a caress which made her shiver. She stared blindly at the framed photographs crowded among the flower arrangement on the marble mantelshelf, her body suddenly boneless, her knees shaking as his mouth moved lower.

Suddenly Catherine stiffened.

'What is it, *meu amor*?' asked Eduardo, looking up at her reflection.

'The photograph,' she whispered, pointing. 'The small one half hidden behind the mirror. Who is it?'

She swallowed drily as Eduardo reached for the snapshot of a darkly handsome youth.

'Who *is* it?' she repeated in anguish.

'It is Pedro when he was a boy,' he said slowly. 'After he was killed Ana put all photographs of him away. This one must have been overlooked. Until now.' Eduardo's breathing quickened as he looked from his brother's face to Catherine's reflection then back again, and convulsively she pushed his encircling arms away and turned round.

'Was there a strong resemblance between Pedro and Isabel?' she asked fearfully, unable to tear her eyes away from the photograph.

Eduardo looked as though someone had dealt him a body blow. '*E verdade*, though until this moment I had not realised it was so marked. Pedro was the only one to follow my mother's family for looks. The rest of us are pure Barroso.'

Their eyes locked in dawning horror as Eduardo's face settled into lines so deep that they looked like scars.

Catherine clasped her shaking hands together. 'You see it too, don't you? *Don't* you?'

His eyes closed for an instant. '*Deus*, Catherine, what are you *saying*?'

She shivered convulsively, and Eduardo swore under his breath, his arms reaching for her, but she shied away.

'*Don't*! Eduardo—can't you see? I may be the image of Isabel to *you*, but the resemblance eluding your aunt and your sisters is to Pedro, which means——' Her voice cracked as they stared at each other in anguish.

'No. *No*.' Eduardo shook his head as if to free it from a vision too unbearable to contemplate. 'It is not true. You cannot be my brother's child!'

Later, as the ancient house creaked and settled itself down for the night, Catherine lay dry-eyed and sleepless in the moonlit darkness. Eduardo's anguished words reverberated over and over again in her ears like a death knell. The moment they were uttered she had tried to run, to escape, but Eduardo had held her fast, forcing brandy through her bloodless lips as he kept her beside him on a sofa. He'd held her icy hand tightly, his face as colourless as hers as at last, with extreme reluctance, he admitted there was a remote possibility that his brother Pedro could have been her father.

The former Conde de Pontalegre had sent his elder son away to travel for a while after Isabel died, hoping that a change of scene would help Pedro recover from his horror and guilt at the girl's suicide. Eduardo was forced to confess that not only had Pedro's travels taken him to England, but also that the time of his visit coincided with the love-affair which resulted in Catherine's birth. To add further weight to the idea Eduardo told her that the Pedro who returned home eventually had changed. The carefree boy was gone forever, replaced by a brooding, solitary man who avoided the company of women, making it plain that any hope of continuing the Barroso line lay solely with Eduardo.

Catherine buried her face in the pillow in despair. If only her mother were at home! When she was young Catherine had respected her mother's wish to keep the identity of her lover secret, but on her twenty-first birthday Catherine demanded the truth. Barbara Ward had finally admitted that he was dead, her request to keep his name secret made with such dignity that Catherine couldn't bring herself to press for more information. But after tonight, she thought in anguish, she badly needed to know the truth, however unpalatable—and whatever the consequences.

Tears soaked her pillow at the thought of her parting with Eduardo.

He'd gazed at her in silence for a long, anguished interval, then raised her cold fingers to his lips. 'This, for us, then, is all,' he said roughly. 'Yet even as I kiss your hand, *querida*, you know, *sem duvida*, that I would give my soul to kiss your mouth.'

Catherine had gazed at him in utter dismay. 'Which cuts right to the heart of the problem, Eduardo. If what we suspect is true it would probably cost us our souls if you did.'

CHAPTER TEN

THE flight to Oporto was uneventful, but this time swollen grey clouds greeted Catherine at the airport. Rain looked imminent as she hurried across the puddled tarmac into the terminal building, where she passed through Customs at even greater speed than on her first visit, emerging to find the same young man from the car-hire company waiting to greet her.

'*Bom dia*, Miss Ward,' he said, smiling. 'You must like our country to return so soon.'

'I do, very much!' Catherine assured him.

In minutes she was on her way again, needing no directions this time as she took the road signposted to Viana do Castelo and Valenca do Minho. But once clear of the airport the heavens opened at last and rain came sheeting down to put paid to any idea about driving to Pontalegre at top speed.

The enforced slowness of the journey left Catherine with far too much time to think. Doubts began to mushroom in her mind as she passed familiar landmarks along the route. Excitement and expectation had buoyed her up during the plane flight, but now that she was actually on the road to Pontalegre Catherine became more certain with every kilometre that she should have taken her mother's advice and told Eduardo she was coming. Five long weeks had elapsed since the agony of their leave-taking that final night. Anything could have happened since then.

She frowned in concentration through the curtain of rain as she negotiated bends in the road with extra care, her nerves knotting as the signpost for Pontalegre came into view. On the last, winding lap of the journey along the River Lima the rain was unrelenting, making driving conditions so difficult that when the boundary walls of Quinta das Lagoas loomed into view Catherine's uneasiness about her reception was forgotten in the relief of having arrived.

Catherine negotiated the car through the arch, then drove round to the back of the house to find the patio deserted except for the battered pick-up. There was no one working in the fields, and no Eduardo to greet her. To her dismay the entire house looked dark and shuttered. She was on the verge of turning tail to head north for Quinta da Floresta and the newly-weds, when a loud cry of greeting hailed her as Fernanda shot from the quarters she shared with her husband, her face beaming with surprise under the scarf thrown over her head.

'Dona Caterina! *Que susto*—what a surprise. But Senhor Eduardo said nothing——'

'He doesn't know. I—I was passing, so I thought I'd call in. I'm afaid I've come uninvited this time.' Catherine jumped from the car to kiss the other woman's cheek. 'Hello, Fernanda, how are you?'

Fernanda assured the unexpected visitor she was well, her welcome reassuringly warm as she shooed Catherine up the steps to the house, apologising for an unlit fire, the rain, her general unpreparedness as she showed Catherine into the hall, which was gloom personified as the rain sheeted down outside. Fernanda rushed around, turning on lights, divesting Catherine of her damp jacket while she talked nineteen to the dozen in English which, although liberally peppered with Portuguese, soon made it clear to Catherine that Eduardo was in Lisbon, and not expected back until the following day.

Catherine, dismayed, suggested she go on to Pontalegre to book a room at the hotel, but the idea shocked Fernanda so much that she dropped the subject hastily, for fear of offering insult to the hospitality of Quinta das Lagoas. Fernanda made it very clear that Catherine was not travelling another metre that day, and put a match to the logs in the fireplace in the great *sala*.

'Rest and get warm while I bring tea, then I shall make ready the room in the tower,' she said firmly.

Catherine sank down on to a sofa, staring at the flames as they curled around the crackling logs, utterly convinced by now that this was a huge, terrible mistake. Since Eduardo wasn't here it might have been better if she'd found no one home at all, then she could have gone on to Pontalegre and contacted Ana from there. Because if Eduardo was in Lisbon he was certain to be with Antonia Soares—as he was perfectly entitled to be.

Fernanda came hurrying back with a tray of tea and the inevitable toast, apologising for the lack of cake.

'Oh, Fernanda, I do apologise for putting you to all this trouble.' Catherine gazed at her in remorse. 'I should have telephoned, asked if it was all right to come.'

Fernanda looked blank. '*Porquê*? You are Ana's friend, and welcome always. Ana and her husband are visiting his parents, so where else should you be but here?'

So there was no escape route via Ana, thought Catherine, depressed, as Fernanda went off to prepare her room. Her mother had warned her about acting on impulse, but the desire to see Eduardo had been so overpowering that in the end she'd booked her flight and come running to him. But somehow it had never occurred to her that he wouldn't be at home. What an idiot! Now she had a whole day to fret herself to fiddlestrings over his reaction to the sight of her, which would probably be nothing like the welcome she'd had from Fernanda. In fact she would hardly blame him if he sent her packing, furious with her because she'd driven away at first light from Casa das Camelias after that terrible night, leaving Eduardo with only a brief note by way of apology.

When Fernanda announced her intention of cooking a special meal Catherine wouldn't hear of it, insisting she'd be perfectly happy with a small portion of whatever dinner was already under way in the housekeeper's private quarters, provided there was enough. Fernanda assured her there was more than enough, but doubted the suitability of the *sarrabulho* she had ready for her husband.

'It is a dish of the region, served much in cold weather,' she explained, worried. 'But it is no more than a *mistura* of chopped meats in a sauce.'

Catherine assured her it sounded wonderful after her plastic snack on the plane, then asked for news of the newly-weds, which occupied a lengthy interval before Fernanda finally escorted her to the beautiful, familiar room in the tower.

'There are no *turistas* at this time of year,' she assured Catherine, 'but do not fear. The bed is aired, and the water is hot. You will enjoy a hot bath after your journey in the rain.'

Catherine thanked her warmly. 'By the way,' she added casually, 'has anyone been engaged to help with the tourists now Ana has gone?'

'No,' said Fernanda, shaking her head. 'Senhor Eduardo has seen many girls, but none pleased him.'

Catherine somehow managed to refrain from hugging Fernanda at the news. 'He must be working very hard, then,' she said sedately.

'He tires himself out,' agreed Fernanda, brightening Catherine even more by telling her that Senhor Eduardo was very *triste* these days and plainly missed Ana very much. He would be very glad to see his visitor, Fernanda promised her, then declared her intention of moving into the house into Ana's old room that night, but Catherine refused to put her to such trouble, assuring her that she had no qualms about sleeping alone at the Quinta das Lagoas.

'Especially since it's only for one night,' she added firmly.

Fernanda looked disappointed. 'One night only? Can you not stay a little longer once Senhor Eduardo returns?'

'If he's so busy he won't have time to spare for uninvited guests,' smiled Catherine, secretly praying she was wrong.

It seemed very strange to shower and dress for her solitary meal, knowing she was alone in the ancient house. But if there were ghosts, thought Catherine, as she dried her hair, they would be the friendly, welcoming Portuguese variety, unlikely to object to the stranger in their midst.

When Fernanda served dinner later at the small table in the great *sala* Catherine persuaded her to stay and chat while the deliciously savoury *sarrabulho* was consumed. To please Fernanda, afterwards she ate a small portion of caramel pudding, then assured the housekeeper that she had plenty of books, knew where to make herself tea if she wanted it, and promised to put out all the lights on the way to bed.

Fernanda took the keys of the car so that her husband Manoel could put it in one of the old stables out of the rain, then left Catherine to her book. The dying log fire gave out a heat which soon made Catherine drowsy after the substantial meal and eventually, her mind too much occupied with thoughts of Eduardo to read, she turned off the lights in the *sala* and the hall and went up to her room.

But as she climbed the spiral stair the vivid memory of the night Eduardo had lain in wait at the top banished her drowsiness completely. Once she was in bed she did her best to read, but her mind refused to grapple with the complexities of the convoluted legal thriller she'd bought at the airport, and eventually she turned off the light and lay gazing at the night sky, which, irritatingly, was clear now, complete with stars and waning moon.

Catherine was half asleep at last when the quiet but unmistakable sound of a car engine roused her. She slid out of bed and went to the window to peer down into the courtyard, her heart banging against her ribs as she saw Eduardo emerge from his car. When no lights went on in Fernanda's quarters Catherine hugged her arms across her chest in an agony of indecision, wondering whether it was better to stay where she was and leave confrontation to the morning, or get it over with straight away. Eventually, knowing she had no hope of sleep now Eduardo was home, she put on her dressing-gown and went outside on the landing.

A faint glimmer of light from below indicated that Eduardo must at least be in this part of the house. Catherine took her courage in both hands and stole down the stairs to the hall, where a shaft of light from the half-open door of the study drew her across the cold flagstones like a magnet. She paused just outside, hardly daring to breathe as she gazed at Eduardo, her heart contracting at the sight of him. He looked thinner and older, his eyes dark-rimmed with fatigue as he studied some papers. After a moment he stiffened, sensing that he was being watched. He swung round menacingly, then stood utterly still, his eyes blank with shock at the sight of her.

'Hello, Eduardo.' She tried to smile. 'Does your offer of a job still stand?'

'*Catherine*?' he said incredulously. He closed his eyes tightly, then opened them again very slowly as though certain he was hallucinating. He started towards her with outstretched arms, then stopped dead, his arms falling to his sides. 'You came to see Ana, perhaps?' he asked, the lines scored deep at the corners of his mouth.

'No.' Catherine's smile wavered. 'I came to see you.'

He passed a hand over his eyes as though her statement was too difficult to take in. '*Perdôe-me*. I do not understand.'

'I'm sorry, Eduardo, I know I should have telephoned first——'

'I have waited for you to telephone ever since you ran away!' he said bitterly. 'At first I spent hours ringing your home.'

'I wasn't there——'

'*Evidentemente*!' He glared at her. 'How could you do such a thing to me, Catherine? I was insane with worry.'

'I never thought you'd try to—to get in touch with me,' she said unhappily. 'I didn't go home, you see. I just couldn't face the thought of waiting there alone until my mother came back, so I slept on a friend's sofa in London so I could go job-hunting.'

They looked at each other in tense silence.

'Why have you come?' he said at last with violence.

'To tell you I'm not Pedro's daughter,' she blurted.

Eduardo's eyes burned darkly as every vestige of colour left his face. '*Como*?' He swallowed hard. 'Say that again!'

'I am not Pedro's daughter, which means I'm not your niece, either,' she pointed out, utterly dampened by his reaction to the news. 'So now I've said what I've come to say, I'll take myself off——'

Eduardo moved suddenly to seize her wrists. '*Estupida*!' he said roughly. 'Tell me how you know this—immediately!' Suddenly he realised she was shivering. 'You are cold. Your wrap is thin. Come. Let us go into the *sala*.' Eduardo's eyes dropped to her bare feet. '*Que loucura*, Catherine! You will catch a chill.' He gave her a crooked smile. 'If what you say is true my immortal soul is no longer in danger if I touch you, *não é*? So I shall carry you.' He scooped her up in his arms and strode with her to the *sala*, kicking the door shut behind him. He set her down on the sofa, then bent to rekindle the dying embers of the fire as she curled up with the offending feet hidden beneath the folds of her kimono. When flames were licking the logs once more Eduardo settled himself on the opposite corner of the sofa, his eyes compelling as they met hers. 'Why has it taken you so long to give me this news?'

'I had the best part of a month to wait before my mother came back before I found out.' She bit her lip. 'At first I thought I'd just write. But that seemed so cold. And I *had* written to you already, Eduardo.'

'*E verdade*,' he said grimly. 'You wrote twice. A note left for me that first morning. Then again from England to thank me so politely for your stay in my house as though you were a stranger. But you gave no address.'

Her eyes fell. 'I—I thought it best not to say where I was.'

'At first I was crazy with worry!' He leaned forward to take her hand in a punishing grip. 'But in time I became convinced that you did not wish to be found. That you did not feel for me as I felt for you.'

'Are you mad?' she said indignantly. 'I couldn't eat, couldn't sleep...' She stopped, suddenly breathless at the leap of heat in his eyes.

'Catherine,' he said urgently, 'tell me what you have learned—unless ...' He paused, eyeing her questioningly. 'Unless you do not wish to betray your mother's confidence, perhaps?'

Catherine relaxed a little. 'It was my mother who said I must tell you. She feels horribly guilty now about keeping me in the dark about my father. And,' she added, smiling wryly, 'she was very cross with me too, I might add.'

'*Porquê?*'

'For being stupid enough to think she'd have let me come here at all if Pedro actually *had* been my father. She said——' She stopped, colouring.

Eduardo's fingers caressed her hand as he moved a little closer. 'What did she say, Catherine?'

'That I must be so much in love, my brain had stopped functioning, otherwise I'd have worked that bit out for myself!'

He laughed, looking suddenly younger and more like the Eduardo of before. 'Is that true, Catherine?'

'If you mean about my non-functioning brain, yes.'

'I did not, but no matter.' His eyes smiled into hers.

Catherine kept to the matter in hand with effort. 'Yes, well—we've established who my father wasn't, but you haven't asked me who he was.'

Eduardo shook his head. 'There is no necessity to tell me this, Catherine. Since your mother has guarded her secret so long perhaps only you should share it. For you alone are my concern. Not your father.'

'Oh, Eduardo—that's a beautiful thing to say!' She smiled incandescently, the light in her wide amber eyes suddenly altogether too much for the iron self-control Eduardo had been exerting.

'I can exist no longer without holding you,' he said roughly, and seized her in his arms, his mouth on hers. They clutched at each other convulsively, hands and lips caressing in a mutual frenzy of thanksgiving for the freedom to express feelings they had believed forbidden to them forever.

'*Deus*,' said Eduardo unsteadily, raising his head at last to look down into her face. 'I cannot believe this is true—that you are really here in my arms like this. When I looked up to see you standing there I thought you were a *fantasma*—a beautiful ghost my longing had conjured up.'

Catherine buried her head against his shoulder. 'I'm no ghost, Eduardo.'

He smoothed an unsteady hand over her silk-covered hip. '*E verdade, meu amor*. You are flesh and blood. And so am I,' he added hoarsely.

Catherine smiled up at him. 'I had noticed.'

His eyes narrowed to a warning glitter. 'Therefore you will go back to your corner, and I will sit as far away as I can endure, so that I may look but not touch.'

'Spoil-sport!' she teased, then sobered. 'In any case, Eduardo, I must tell you about my father before we go any further——' She stopped dead, blushing to the roots of her hair. 'I mean ...'

'I know well what you mean,' he assured her caressingly, and captured her hand. 'I think we may allow ourselves to hold hands, *não é*?'

Catherine was glad of his hard, possessive clasp as she told him how shocked Barbara Ward had been at the sight of her haggard, unhappy daughter. The moment she learned the reason for Catherine's misery she gave her the truth at last, confessing that her shame and guilt over a love-affair with a boy half her age had cut so deep that she could never bring herself to reveal his identity.

'As I suspected all along,' said Catherine, 'her lover was a pupil at the school where she was assistant matron. But Mother's exaggerating a bit to say that he was half her age. He was nineteen, she was thirty-one.'

Tom Wilde was an American. Before entry into Harvard he was sent by his Anglophile father to study in England for a year. He was a brilliant student, good at games, physically attractive and popular with peers and staff alike. Then just before he was due to fly home for good he went down with raging influenza.

The school was ready to close, the rest of the staff eager to get away for their summer holidays. Barbara Ward, who had nothing planned for the summer vacation, volunteered to stay behind to nurse the invalid and see him off on his plane once he was well enough to travel.

'I could see she found it hard to go on at this point,' said Catherine quietly. 'It seems they were together in complete isolation for three weeks. He was a very mature boy, she was a very attractive woman. The inevitable happened.'

Eduardo frowned in sympathy. 'But why did your mother not tell you this before?'

'Mother was brought up a devout Catholic. To seduce a pupil in the very school where she worked was a sin of such enormity to her that she could never bring herself to talk of it to anyone, least of all me.'

'Since I am sure your mother was beautiful, and this Tom Wilde was a normal, healthy boy of nineteen,' observed Edurado drily, 'I doubt very much that seduction was necessary.'

Catherine smiled ruefully. 'You've got a point. The bunch I knew in college weren't exactly shy!'

He laughed. '*E verdade*—I was a student once myself, remember! But your mother,' he added. 'Why did she never tell him about you? Was marriage completely out of the question?'

'I'm sure it never entered her head. He was young, clever, with a brilliant career in front of him. Mother could never have ruined all that for him. Besides,' she added, 'she felt—still feels—that she was totally to blame.'

'And now?' said Eduardo gently. 'Does your mother know anything about this young father of yours, *querida*? Whether he achieved this brilliant career?'

'That's the sad part. Instead of going to Harvard he went against his father's wishes and enlisted in the army as soon as he got back to the States. He wrote to Mother en route to Vietnam. Eventually she heard from the matron of the school that he'd been killed in action.'

Eduardo raised her hand to his, kissing her hand in wordless sympathy. 'A tragic waste of a young life.'

'Just like Isabel,' agreed Catherine sadly, then jumped up. 'Which reminds me.'

'Where are you going?' he demanded, frowning.

'I brought something for you to see. It's up in the bedroom. I'll just slip up and get it.'

'No, Catherine!' he said, springing up. 'It does not do to run about this house barefoot at this time of the year. I shall carry you.'

'It's too far,' she protested, 'and I'm too heavy——'

'*Bobagem*,' said Eduardo firmly, picking her up. 'But do not argue—I shall need my breath for the journey!'

By the time Eduardo deposited her on her feet in her room he was breathing hard, his chest rising and falling rapidly as he leaned in the open doorway, Catherine only marginally less breathless herself.

'I told you I was heavy!' she protested.

'This was not the only problem,' he informed her unevenly. 'Merely to hold you in my arms again does strange things to my entire system, *meu amor.*'

Their eyes met and held before she turned away hurriedly to rummage in her suitcase. She slid a large leather-bound bible from a padded envelope, and handed it to him expectantly.

Eduardo eyed it in surprise. 'A bible! You intend to improve my mind, *querida*?'

'No. Just to clear up a little mystery.' Catherine smiled at him tantalisingly. 'After all, there's still the little mystery of this face of mine, remember. When I told my mother it was the basis of our fears about Pedro she dismissed it as pure coincidence. Apparently I look just like my grandmother did when she was young. *And,*' she added mysteriously, 'my grandmother followed *her* mother for looks.'

Eduardo stared at her blankly. 'I do not see——'

'You will, you will.' Catherine smiled teasingly. 'I may not be your niece, Eduardo Barroso, but a visit to your aunt Clara confirmed beyond all shadow of doubt that I happen to be your cousin a couple of times removed!'

Eduardo stared at her dumbfounded, then let Catherine pull him over to the bed to sit beside her.

'When I told Mother Miss Holroyd was interested in my family tree she produced an old suitcase full of family papers. This was at the bottom.' Catherine smiled up into Eduardo's intent face. 'I don't know whether it's the same in Portugal, but in England people quite often used the family bible to record births, deaths and marriages, and so on.'

The bible fell open on Catherine's knee where a black ribbon marked the page recording the most recent events in the Ward family.

'There,' she said, pointing. 'The last entries in the book, the deaths quite close to each other of Bridget and George Ward, my grandparents. Before that there's the birth of Catherine Sarah Ward, that's me, and before that the birth of Barbara Sarah, my mother. But here comes the interesting bit.' She smiled up at Eduardo in triumph as she turned back to the page which recorded the deaths and marriage of the owners of the bible—her great-grandparents Patrick Mahoney and his wife Sarah, whose maiden name, written in faded ink but perfectly legible still, was Holroyd.

'Holroyd!' exclaimed Eduardo. He turned to Catherine in delight. 'Then you are blood of my blood already, *meu amor*!'

She smiled incandescently. 'But you don't know how, yet.'

'Does it matter?' he said, his urge to kiss her so evident that Catherine moved away hastily, determined to finish her story.

After her discovery Catherine had immediately got in touch with Clara Holroyd and went off to stay with her in Warwick, taking the bible with her. 'Your aunt was delighted,' she said, chuckling. 'It proved she was right, as usual. And she knew all about Sarah Holroyd, would you believe! Apparently my great-grandmother was the skeleton in the Holroyd closet!'

'*Como*?' said Eduardo, laughing.

'She was the family scandal, you foreigner!'

'Here you are the foreigner,' he reminded her with dignity, then planted a determined kiss on her mouth by way of apology. 'Go on.'

Miss Holroyd had taken great relish in telling Catherine about her father's flighty cousin Sarah, who ran off with a jockey by the name of Paddy Mahoney, and was never heard from again.

'Apparently your aunt Clara was too young at the time to know much about it, except for a lot of whispering behind closed doors,' said Catherine, as she leaned against Eduardo's shoulder, giggling. 'Actually, if you look at the dates, you'll see my grandmother arrived in the world rather too soon after the naughty Sarah's wedding—in fact, one way and another, my family history's decidedly "iffy" from way back. Do you mind having a rather questionable connection like me for a cousin?'

'Since you are to be my wife, not my cousin, it is of no consequence,' he informed her casually.

Catherine's jaw dropped. She clamped it together again, trying to hide her ecstatic reaction to his matter-of-fact statement. 'Hey! You're taking things a bit for granted, Eduardo Barroso. I came back here to see if you still had a job for me, that's all.'

'You lie, Catherine,' he said softly, taking her hand in his. His eyes held an unsettling gleam as he rhythmically smoothed his thumb over her palm. 'The original plan, *não é*, was to work together as a means of getting to know each other better.'

She frowned. 'Well, yes. But I thought that was to be a sort of run-up to becoming lovers, not married.'

'It is possible to be both!'

'You don't really know me well enough——' she began, but he laid a finger on her lips, silencing her.

'We were together for two weeks, we have been parted for five more. This has been enough—more than enough—to show me that I do not wish to be parted from you again. Ever.' He raised her hand to his mouth, his lips warm against her palm. 'I think you care for me a little, Catherine. Otherwise you would not be here.'

'You know perfectly well that I care for you a lot,' she said crossly. 'So much so that the day I left here, thinking I'd never see you again, I finally understood exactly why poor Isabel committed suicide.'

With a smothered sound Eduardo pulled her against him, holding her face against his chest as he smoothed her hair. 'But I do not wish you to die for me, *meu amor*. I want you to live for me, to live *with* me, for the rest of our lives.' He turned her face up to his. 'Will you bring yourself to forsake your beloved Inglaterra to make your home here with me in Portugal?'

'I could only do it for you,' Catherine said simply. 'But whatever doubts I might have had before, the past few weeks have taught me that wherever you are, Eduardo, is exactly where I want to be.'

'Why?'

'*Why*?'

Eduardo nodded, his eyes narrowed to an unsettling dark glitter. 'I am enchanted to learn your desire for my company, *sem duvida*. But now I wish you to tell me the exact reason for this.'

She scowled. 'I thought I had.'

'Ah, but you have omitted to say the three most important words in any language, English or Portugese,' he said softly, and touched her lower lip with the tip of his finger. 'You know *I* love *you*,

Catherine, because I have told you so before, and will continue to tell you so while there is breath left in my body.'

'Why do you think I came back to you like this?' she said unsteadily, utterly ravished by this statement as he flattened a hand against her back to draw her closer. 'Once I knew the truth I just came running to you whether you wanted me or not, risking rejection, or, even worse, of finding you married to Antonia——'

'You ran no risk of either,' he interrupted, his lips a hair's breadth from hers. 'How could you think I would reject you, *querida*?'

Catherine found it hard to think of anything at the moment other than the fact that she wanted him to make love to her. 'You—you've been to Lisbon,' she said raggedly. 'Weren't you with Antonia?'

'Yes. We dined together last night.' Eduardo's lips moved delicately along the line of her jaw. 'So that she could give me her wedding gift for Ana.'

'Oh.' Catherine closed her eyes, shivering, as his lips began to move back towards her mouth. 'Was that the only reason?'

'No. I invariably dine with Antonia when I am in Lisbon. She was once my colleague, you may remember.'

'I find it very hard to forget,' said Catherine through her teeth.

Eduardo shook her slightly. 'Open your eyes,' he commanded.

She obeyed, trembling as she met the look in his.

'You,' said Eduardo, in a tone she'd never heard before, 'are all the woman I want, now and forever, Catherine. Do you believe me?'

She gave a long, shaky sigh, and buried her head against his shoulder. 'Yes, Eduardo.'

'Then tell me you love me.'

'I know I'm stupid, but it's hard to say in cold blood,' she whispered.

He gave a smothered groan. 'You are fortunate your blood is cold! Mine burns.' And suddenly Eduardo pushed her down on the bed and began to kiss her with a starving desperation which made nonsense of her talk of cold blood. The very first touch of his mouth on hers spread liquid fire curling from the pit of her stomach through her veins, making her heart hammer and her pulse race. Their breath mingled together in great gasps as his hands sought her breasts and his mouth moved from her face to her throat, then suddenly Eduardo heaved himself up, balanced with a hand either side of her boneless, abandoned body, his eyes glittering with unspoken demand.

'I love you,' she said hoarsely. 'You know I love you.' Closing her eyes, she held up her arms in mute appeal which Eduardo answered in a way which put an end to any talk for a long, impassioned interval. At last he tore his mouth away from hers and tried to dislodge her clinging arms.

'*Meu amor*, I must go,' Eduardo panted. 'Now. You do not understand——'

'You're right. I don't.' She gazed at him imploringly. 'Why must you go? I want you to stay, darling. Please.'

Eduardo groaned like a man in pain. 'But if I stay you know what will happen.'

Catherine's hands fell away. She rolled over, hiding her face in the counterpane.

There was a silence.

'I want to make love to you so much, I am in torment,' he said at last, his voice shaking. 'But I wish to prove to you that it is not only your body I desire, to wait until you are my wife before——'

'You haven't actually asked me to marry you yet.' Catherine sat up, pushing her heavy hair away from her face, unshed tears in her eyes.

Eduardo gazed at her in silence for a long, charged interval, then, with a total lack of self-consciousness, he went down on one knee beside the bed and raised her hand to his lips. 'Catherine Sarah Ward, will you be my wife?' he asked formally.

Catherine let out a great, unsteady sigh. 'Oh, yes, Eduardo, I will!' she assured him, and smiled, the tears spilling at last down her cheeks.

'Do not cry, *meu amor*!' He leapt to sit beside her on the bed, kissing her eyelids shut, his tongue on the salt of her tears. Their lips met and clung, then he drew back a little to gaze in question into her radiant face, before drawing back the covers to lay her against the pillows. He smoothed the kimono away from her shoulders, his hands suddenly shaking as he peeled away her nightgown. She moved restlessly as he gazed at her in silence for a moment, his scrutiny as tactile as a caress. Suddenly he tore at his tie, and she scrambled to her knees to help him, both of them on fire with the need to be in each other's arms at last with every barrier gone.

Catherine sensed that Eduardo's intention had been to make love to her with all the subtlety and restraint at his command. But as their bodies came together in naked contact for the first time he was as helpless as she at the wonder of it, unable to maintain a control stretched to breaking-point by the weeks of agonised separation. Within seconds their wild kisses and caresses added fuel to a fire which overwhelmed them in a mutual, overriding surge of heat and longing. All the misery and frustration of the past few weeks melted in the fierce flame which cauterised her fleeting stab of pain, then consumed them both in a blaze of glory which left them clinging to each other in speechless wonder as it died slowly away.

'I could not wait. Forgive me. It was the tears,' said Eduardo hoarsely. 'Also you misled me——'

'Forgive?' interrupted Catherine, puzzled.

'I am not normally so—so precipitate? Is this the word?'

Catherine tried to push him away. 'The word I object to is "normally"! I don't want to know about your other women——'

He held her fast, laughing deep in his throat. 'I am a man, not a boy, *querida*. Would you have me a virgin?'

She shook her head, avoiding his eyes as she smoothed her tumbled hair.

He propped himself up on one elbow, his gaze proprietorial as it wandered over her heavy eyes and flushed face. They lingered on her mouth for a moment, then he bent his head to kiss her lingeringly, his free hand smoothing the curve of her cheek. 'But you lied, *meu amor*,' he said with deep satisfaction. 'You have had no lover before.'

'I didn't lie. I told you often enough in fact!' Catherine eyed him militantly. 'When you overheard my conversation with Ana you jumped to conclusions, Eduardo Barroso. I warned her not to expect too much because of tales I'd heard from other girls, not from experience. I told you Dan and I were just boy-and-girl stuff. He liked other people to think we slept together, but—but I wouldn't. That's why he dumped me in the end.'

Eduardo crushed her close. 'How could you love such a man?'

Catherine hugged him back, rubbing her cheek against his. 'I only *thought* I did. I never really knew what love was until I met you, Eduardo.'

With a muffled sound he sought her mouth, kissing her in passionate acknowledgement of her words before he put her away a little to look down into her face. 'Tell me. You believed you loved this boy. Were you truly never tempted to become his lover?'

'Sometimes,' she said honestly. 'But not only was I convent-educated, like Isabel, I also had the ultimate deterrent in my mother's experience. Not that she ever lectured me about avoiding the mistake she made. She didn't need to. If ever I was the slightest bit tempted to give in I thought of what happened to her, and that was that.'

Eduardo smoothed back her hair, smiling crookedly. 'Had you no thought of her tonight?'

Catherine stared at him, arrested. 'Heavens, no. No, I didn't. All I could think of was you.'

'*Meu amor!*' He kissed her lingeringly, then settled back with a sigh, her head on his shoulder. 'Tonight when I returned from Lisbon the world was a desert. Life held no hope of happiness for me.'

Catherine stretched luxuriously against him, her arm thrown across his waist. 'And now?'

'And now I have everything in the world my heart could desire.' He gave a sudden, joyous laugh as he glanced at the bedside table. 'Including an alarm clock, I see!'

'What's so great about my alarm clock?'

'Because, having experienced the bliss of your bed tonight, *querida*, I have no intention of seeking my own a moment before I must!'

Catherine giggled. 'You mean you're going to dash down to your room at the crack of dawn and rumple your bed before Fernanda arrives?'

'*E verdade*,' he said with feeling. 'Can you imagine her wrath if she found me here with you like this?'

Catherine shuddered. 'Perhaps you'd better go to sleep right now, then, to make sure you wake up in time.'

'Ah.' He shook with laughter against her. 'The alarm clock is a safeguard only. It was not my intention to sleep all night, *meu amor*.'

'Oh.' Catherine felt her cheeks burn in the darkness. 'I thought maybe you were tired.'

'With you in my arms like this, how could I be? *Se Deus quizer*, there will be countless nights for us to sleep together,' he assured her, turning her face up to his. 'The first night I wish to stay awake every minute until dawn, thanking God for the miracle of having you here in my arms.'

Catherine kissed him ardently. 'What a beautiful thing to say.'

'It is the truth, *querida*!'

She rubbed her cheek against his. 'My mother will be so pleased, darling. She was desperately sorry for causing us pain like that.'

'Perhaps it was necessary,' he said soberly. 'Our enforced parting, bitter though it was, made it clear how much we care for each other, *não é*?'

'Very true!'

'Tia Clara will be pleased also.' Eduaro laughed. 'She places much emphasis on the Old Alliance between Portugal and England.'

Catherine propped herself up on an elbow to smile at him. 'Do you want our alliance to produce a son?'

Eduardo's answering smile quickened her pulse. 'If God is good I would like a son, *naturalmente*, a daughter also. But never doubt that I count myself fortunate among men just to have you for my wife, *querida*.'

In response to such a gratifying sentiment Catherine leaned down to kiss him, and Eduardo's arms reached up to pull her down to him in an embrace which put an end to any thought of sleep. Dawn came all too quickly as the shrill sound of her alarm signalled that it was time for him to leave.

Eduardo threw on his clothes hastily, smiling into her heavy eyes.

'I wish you could stay,' she said drowsily.

He sat down on the edge of the bed to take her hand. 'I also.' He kissed her fingers one by one. 'I shall move heaven and earth to arrange our marriage as soon as humanly possible.'

Catherine smiled. 'You never answered my question, by the way.'

'What question?'

'When I arrived I asked if the job was still open.'

'You wish to work with me?'

'Of course.' Her eyes narrowed in warning. 'You don't think I'm going to let some other woman spend so much time with you!'

'You are jealous! I am glad. Also I shall be delighted to have you work at my side,' he added, grinning.

Catherine stretched luxuriously beneath the covers. 'Our alliance will be practical, believe me—I see no point in wasting good money on some other woman's wages.'

Eduardo kissed her nose. 'What a wife you will make, Catherine!'

The first rays of sunshine highlighted a wicked gold gleam in her eyes. 'Inexperienced, but willing!'

'The perfect wife,' he agreed, a smile twitching the corners of his mouth. 'Otherwise, you understand, I would not have chosen you.'

She sat bolt upright, laughing, but he silenced her protest with a caressing forefinger on her lips.

'I am so happy, I cannot help but tease a little.' He raised both her hands to his and kissed them. 'And since you will, *sem duvida*, be the perfect wife, I shall strive to be a good husband, Catherine. Our marriage, I make you my vow, will be the happiest alliance of all.'

PORTUGAL

Portugal is a country which has always conjured up pictures of beautiful, sandy beaches and tumble-down Roman ruins together with vineyards and quaint fishing villages—what better place to dream of romance?

Certainly, Portugal in the twentieth century remains relatively unspoiled, despite becoming popular with tourists in recent years. Yet it remains a country of contrasts—from the varied sights of its capital, Lisbon, to the old-world simplicity of country fairs where you can buy delicately made cotton blouses, handicrafts and, if your heart desires, even flocks of brightly painted Barcelos clay roosters, renowned as the emblem of Portugal!

THE ROMANTIC PAST

Today, Lisbon has a population of 1.5 million but nevertheless remains a sun-struck place with low-rise pastel buildings. Indeed, in which other city could you be woken by a cock's crow? Yet this homely nature contrasts with the exotic features of a city built down seven hills which afford dramatic views of buildings embossed with beautifully pat-

terned colour tiles and pavements decorated by
mosaics. According to legend, Lisbon was founded
by Ulysses, and its harbour was referred to as
Ulyssibona on a number of old maps. According to
historians, however, Lisbon was originally a trading
centre called Alis Ubo. The Romans named the city
Felicita Julia and built many public baths, theatres
and tombs; some of these ruins can still be seen
today.

THE ROMANTIC PRESENT—pastimes for lovers…

The capital today remains an ideal place for lovers
who enjoy a city with plenty of variety and interesting sights. For those who enjoy strolling together
hand in hand, many of the city's tree-lined streets
are so twisting that they are often too steep for
cars—what could be more romantic? The elegant
squares and cafés are full of the smell of fresh
flowers—and then there's the local custom of
cooking sardines on outdoor grills! Portugal
manages to combine the exotic with the best of
simplicity…

Together with enjoying the local fare at street-side
cafés and sampling the Portuguese table wines
such as **Mateus Rosé**, there is plenty to see and
do. For those who are keen gardeners, Portugal is
famous for its stately setting, and, in Lisbon, one
should not miss the **Botanical Garden** with its
stately avenue of royal palms.

One should also try and fit in a visit to the **Castelo de Sâo Jorge**, again in the capital. This was first rebuilt by Afonso Henriques, Portugal's first king, and then, at the end of the sixteenth century, a new royal palace was built on the river front. Today, visitors can enjoy eating a leisurely lunch there followed by a walk through the gardens where white peacocks wander round or simply preen themselves beneath the olive trees.

For those who enjoy a quieter pace of life, where better to go than to visit the **Minho** region in the north-west of Portugal where sleepy villages abound and the pace of life is very different? Indeed, the **Minho** region has been described by some as Portugal's Garden of Eden with its rich soil and plentiful thermal springs—an ideal way to relax after the slightly more hectic pace of the country fairs. Indeed, the fairs are a great way to experience both the friendliness of the lcoals and the mild climate which Portugal is blessed with for the majority of the year.

But, wherever you go in Portugal, if you enjoy good food with deliciously fresh ingredients a meal out is a definite must! Fish is always plentiful and provides the basis for many Portuguese specialities, while you can also enjoy home-made soups such as the *caldo verde*, a thick potato and cabbage soup, or *lampreia*—river eel! Pork is also very popular and is accompanied by *pão de milho* (corn bread) or the more traditional *broa*, a rather more chewy type of bread.

To finish off your meal, you can indulge in either a *crème caramel* or a variety of sweets and cakes together with excellent coffee.

DID YOU KNOW THAT:

* the Portuguese language is ultimately derived from Latin but has also had some Arabic influences. The second language in Portugal is considered to be French although English is rapidly catching up
* Portugal **exports** a variety of items, not only the usual pottery and textiles but also port wine, olive oil and sardines
* the Portuguese **currency** is the *escudo*
* When someone in Portugal says '*Eu te amo*' OR '*Eu te adoro*', they are saying that they love you!

RUGGED. SEXY. HEROIC.

OUTLAWS and HEROES

Stony Carlton—A lone wolf determined never to be tied down.

Gabriel Taylor—Accused and found guilty by small-town gossip.

Clay Barker—At Revenge Unlimited, he *is* the law.

JOAN JOHNSTON, DALLAS SCHULZE and **MALLORY RUSH**, three of romance fiction's biggest names, have created three unforgettable men—modern heroes who have the courage to fight for what is right....

OUTLAWS AND HEROES—available in September wherever Harlequin books are sold.

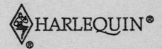

HARLEQUIN®

MILLION DOLLAR SWEEPSTAKES (III)

HARLEQUIN ROMANCE®

brings you

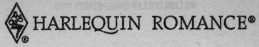

A letter has played an important role in all our romances
in our Sealed with a Kiss series so far, but next month's
THE BEST FOR LAST by Stephanie Howard is a story
with a difference—

All her adult life Cassandra Redmund had kept a diary.
It had detailed the disastrous ending to her relationship
with Damon Grey years before and, now, her present
predicament.

She had run into him again on a Caribbean island
paradise only to discover that Damon's charm was as
persuasive as ever—and just as dangerous. She was
determined she wouldn't give in…but was Cassandra's
fate about to be sealed with a kiss?

Available wherever Harlequin books are sold.

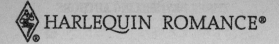

HARLEQUIN ROMANCE®

brings you

Romances that take the family to heart!

A FAMILY CLOSENESS by Emma Richmond

If Davina's fiancé hadn't run off with her best friend, she wouldn't have got involved with Joel Gilman. And now, four years after their disastrous encounter, it seemed that time hadn't dulled their mutual attraction! But Joel had a new woman in his life now—his young daughter, Ammy. And when he asked her to look after the little girl, Davina had a temporary chance to experience what might have been—and what she'd always wanted....

Coming next month, from the bestselling author of
MORE THAN A DREAM!

FT-3

THREE BESTSELLING AUTHORS

HEATHER GRAHAM POZZESSERE
THERESA MICHAELS
MERLINE LOVELACE

bring you

THREE HEROES THAT DREAMS ARE MADE OF!

The Highwayman—He knew the honorable thing was to send his captive home, but how could he let the beautiful Lady Kate return to the arms of another man?

The Warrior—Raised to protect his tribe, the fierce Apache warrior had little room in his heart until the gentle Angie showed him the power and strength of love.

The Knight—His years as a mercenary had taught him many skills, but would winning the hand of a spirited young widow prove to be his greatest challenge?

Don't miss these **UNFORGETTABLE RENEGADES!**

Available in August wherever Harlequin books are sold.

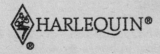HARLEQUIN®

RUGGED. SEXY. HEROIC.

OUTLAWS and HEROES

Stony Carlton—A lone wolf determined never to be tied down.

Gabriel Taylor—Accused and found guilty by small-town gossip.

Clay Barker—At Revenge Unlimited, he *is* the law.

JOAN JOHNSTON, DALLAS SCHULZE and MALLORY RUSH, three of romance fiction's biggest names, have created three unforgettable men—modern heroes who have the courage to fight for what is right....

OUTLAWS AND HEROES—available in September wherever Harlequin books are sold.

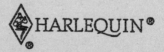

As a Privileged Woman, you'll be entitled to all these *Free Benefits.* And *Free Gifts,* too.

To thank you for buying our books, we've designed an exclusive FREE program called *PAGES & PRIVILEGES*™. You can enroll with just one Proof of Purchase, and get the kind of luxuries that, until now, you could only read about.

*B*IG HOTEL DISCOUNTS

A privileged woman stays in the finest hotels. And so can you—at up to 60% off! Imagine standing in a hotel check-in line and watching as the guest in front of you pays $150 for the same room that's only costing you $60. Your *Pages & Privileges* discounts are good at Sheraton, Marriott, Best Western, Hyatt and thousands of other fine hotels all over the U.S., Canada and Europe.

*F*REE DISCOUNT TRAVEL SERVICE

A privileged woman is always jetting to romantic places. When you fly, just make one phone call for the lowest published airfare at time of booking—or double the difference back! PLUS—

you'll get a $25 voucher to use the first time you book a flight AND 5% cash back on every ticket you buy thereafter through the travel service!

HR-PP3A